The First Tim

The Second Ghost

A Brand New Novel from *New York Times* Bestselling Author

Jessica Beck

GHOST CAT 2: BID FOR MIDNIGHT

Books by Jessica Beck

The Donut Mysteries

Glazed Murder
Fatally Frosted
Sinister Sprinkles
Evil Éclairs
Tragic Toppings
Killer Crullers
Drop Dead Chocolate
Powdered Peril
Illegally Iced
Deadly Donuts

The Classic Diner Mysteries

A Chili Death
A Deadly Beef
A Killer Cake
A Baked Ham
A Bad Egg

The Ghost Cat Cozy Mysteries

Ghost Cat: Midnight Paws
Ghost Cat 2: Bid for Midnight

Jessica Beck is the *New York Times* Bestselling Author of
the
Donut Mysteries
as well as
The Classic Diner Mystery Series
and
The Ghost Cat Cozy Mysteries.

To Mac, the cat who wouldn't take no for an answer!

GHOST CAT 2: BID FOR MIDNIGHT Copyright © 2013
Jessica Beck

All rights reserved.

No part of this book may be reproduced, scanned, or distributed in any printed or electronic form without permission. Please do not participate in or encourage piracy of copyrighted materials in violation of the author's rights. This is a work of fiction. Names, characters, places, and incidents either are the product of the author's imagination or are used fictitiously, and any resemblance to actual persons, living or dead, business establishments, events, or locales is entirely coincidental.

Chapter 1

I knew that something was wrong the second I spotted the ghost of my cat Midnight moving among the boxes at the auction.
It wasn't Midnight's presence that threw me off, though.
It was the fact that he wasn't alone.
A ghostly young woman hovered beside him, just as eerily translucent. It was the first human ghost I'd ever seen in my life, but I had no trouble recognizing her.
That's when I realized that things were about to get a lot more complicated.

Chapter 2

I never dreamed that I would be dragged into another murder investigation by the ghost of my cat Midnight at the estate auction at Silas Bentley's farm, but that's exactly what happened on a crisp Spring morning in Noble Point, North Carolina, when I decided that it was time to add a little new inventory to my eclectic curiosity shop, Memories and Dreams. My name's Christy Blake, and if I'd had *any* say in the matter, I wouldn't have gotten involved, but clearly Midnight had other plans. That cat had been difficult enough to ignore while he'd been alive; becoming an apparition hadn't made him any less determined to get his own way. Shadow, my living cat, and I had learned long ago that we crossed Midnight at our own peril, and his change in status after crossing into the afterlife hadn't affected that in the least.

But I'm getting ahead of myself.

In the beginning, it had all started out innocently enough, but in the end, I probably should have known better.

"Thanks for coming to the auction with me this morning," I told Lincoln Hayes as he drove his truck deeper into the countryside outside town. Lincoln was a local attorney and, more importantly to me, the man who was currently doing his best to woo me. I was in my mid-twenties, and I had no desire to settle down, but Lincoln was determined to make his case, and I wasn't about to shut him out completely. He was too handsome, too much fun to be around, and far too attentive to discard out of hand. Marybeth, my roommate from college and now my landlord as well, had dated Lincoln in high school, but their relationship had evolved into an easy friendship, and now Lincoln had set his sights on me.

"I'm happy to do it. I love a good auction as much as the next man, but this one's kind of special to me," Lincoln said.

He glanced over at me as he added with a smile, "Are you sure that you didn't invite me just because I have an old pickup truck you can use to haul your finds back to your shop?"

"It wasn't the *only* reason, but I won't lie to you," I said. "It did cross my mind. That doesn't hurt your feelings, does it?"

"Why should it? I love Frannie, and I like to take her out every time I get the chance," he said as he lightly stroked the truck's dashboard.

"Why do you call your truck by a woman's name?" I asked him as we got closer to the farm.

"What was I supposed to call her, Butch?"

I laughed off his comment as I took in the landscape around us. The sun was barely up, there was still mist hovering in the fields as we drove past, but we were getting an early start for a good reason. I was only closing Memories and Dreams until noon, and I wanted to get to the auction site ahead of the crowds to scope out the lots that were going to be for sale that morning. While I was certain that many folks would be coming for Silas's vast antique-tool collection, I was there for his late wife Ginny's things, and some of his daughter Summer's possessions as well. Ginny had been a longtime accumulator of the cheap and gaudy, and I was hoping to restock my inventory with some of her baubles. In fact, my old boss, Cora, had tried to buy them earlier, but Summer had wanted everything for herself, and I couldn't really blame her. It was terrible that a gas heater had killed Summer and Silas the month before, carbon monoxide overwhelming them both in the middle of the night, but the *real* tragedy was the fact that Summer had moved back home recently from Charlotte just to help her father out on the farm, a decision that had ultimately cost her her life.

I couldn't allow myself to dwell on the unfortunate circumstances of their deaths, though. A great many of my customers came by the shop every week or two to see what was new, and I was afraid that if I didn't offer them a constantly changing selection of goods, I'd lose them, and I couldn't afford that. Cora had left me majority ownership of the place, but I had to work hard if I was going to keep the doors open for the five years she had dictated in her will in order to retain possession of the shop. I hadn't added anything new since Cora and Midnight had been murdered there, and it was time to embrace my new role in life. I still missed the warm presence of my cat near me, but Midnight had stuck around after what had happened despite all odds and conventional wisdom; I was thankful that I still had a part of him every time he mysteriously appeared to me, but I never knew if the next time he showed up would be the last.

"Christy, did you hear what I just said?" Lincoln asked, pulling me back to our conversation.

"Sorry, my mind was somewhere else," I said. "No, you're right. I suppose Butch would be a ridiculous name for your truck."

"That's all I'm saying," Lincoln replied with a smile. "Are you really going to all this trouble just to buy a few boxes of junk?"

"I'd resent that if it weren't true," I said with a grin. "But there's something you need to remember. One woman's junk is another woman's treasure. Men are just as bad at amassing things they probably don't need, and we both know it."

"I wouldn't deny it for one second," he said with a laugh. "I have my eyes on a pitchfork of Silas's that I'd love to own."

"Do you have a reason to move a lot of hay these days, Lincoln?" I asked him with a gentle grin.

"Not for quite a while, but who knows what the future might hold? Christy, you don't know this about me, but I worked for Silas an entire summer when I was in junior high school, and one of the things I did was help him put up his hay. I've never worked so hard in my life, but I learned a lot that summer, and that pitchfork and I spent a great deal of time together."

"Lincoln, there's nothing wrong with being sentimental," I

said.

"I think so, too, but I'm not all that sure that Silas would have agreed with you, at least not out loud. He was a practical man in most matters, but there was a strong sense of sentiment in him as well; you just had to dig down pretty deep for it."

"Well, from the flyer I read about the auction, it wasn't buried all *that* far down. After all, he and his daughter both kept his wife's costume jewelry, and she's been gone ten years."

"Silas loved Ginny with a great deal of passion, and he doted on Summer, too," Lincoln said. "I hope you get some good pieces today."

"That's why we brought your truck. I'm counting on scoring big. I'll tell you what. I'll even buy that pitchfork for you if you'd like; you've been a really good sport about the whole thing."

"As much as I appreciate the offer, I can't accept it. It's important that I spend money that I earned myself. Do you understand?"

"Perfectly," I said. "I love how that works out sometimes."

He glanced over at me. "What do you mean?"

"I made you an offer, but you politely refused it. I get all of the credit for the thought, but I don't have to crack my wallet open to follow through. That's a big win in my book any day."

"You're something else; you know that, don't you?" he asked with the hint of a grin.

"Something good, I hope," I said.

"I'd say so," he said, and then Lincoln whistled softly to himself. "Would you look at that?"

I looked where he was pointing, and I was alarmed to see that Silas's field closest to the road was already nearly full of pickup trucks, SUVs, and just about every other type of vehicle there was.

Evidently I wasn't the only one who'd decided to get an early peek at what was being offered for auction that day.

"Do you want to split up, or should I just tag along with you?" Lincoln asked me after we registered at a long table in front of the old farmhouse and got our bidding cards. My number was one hundred fifty-seven, and Lincoln was one fifty-eight. We weren't the last ones, either; there was a long line behind us waiting to register as soon as we were finished.

"Either way is fine with me," I said absently as I hunted for the treasures that I knew had to be there.

I glanced over and saw Lincoln smiling at me. "Tell you what. I'm going to walk over to the barn, and you can scout through the boxes in the house. We'll meet up later, okay?"

"It's a deal," I said, and I was quickly on my way.

I hurried into the house and found a crowd there already. This wasn't going to be as easy as I'd hoped, but after I got a look at several of the boxes overflowing with Ginny's possessions, I wanted to win at least a few of them desperately. They were *exactly* what I'd been looking for, and I wasn't going to walk away empty-handed if I could help it. We weren't allowed to go through the treasures, but I could see enough on top to make them interesting to me. The boxes happened to be sitting on a table near the heater that had killed Silas and Summer, and I marveled at how such an innocent-looking household appliance that most folks never noticed could be a silent killer.

"Christy Blake, I don't even know why you're here. This is clearly all just junk," an angry little woman I recognized said the moment she spotted me drooling over one of the boxes of gaudy trinkets. Her first name was Lucy, but I didn't have a clue what her last name might be. I'd seen her in my shop a time or two, but she'd never made much of an impression on me one way or the other. Lucy added with a hint of scorn in her voice, "This entire box isn't worth a dollar."

I laughed, which immediately brought a frown to her face. "I don't know about that," I said. "I'll probably go quite a bit higher than that." I could just see the top layer of jewelry, but I liked what I saw. In each box, there was a layer of newspaper separating the levels, so no one could be exactly sure about what they were getting, since we weren't allowed to dig through the boxes hunting for treasure.

"You'll be a fool if you pay more than a buck," Lucy said angrily.

I decided not to let her spoil my mood. "Well, it won't be the first time." I made it a point to stare at the box in question a little longer, just to rattle her a little. Making a careful note of the number, I brushed past the angry little woman as I said, "Have a nice day, and good luck with your bidding."

"Luck's got nothing to do with it," she answered with a frown.

"Lucy, come over here and look at this," a pale, thin woman in her late fifties said as she grabbed my combatant's arm.

"Myra, let go of me. I'll be with you in a minute."

"If she won't go with you, I'd *love* to see what you found, Myra," I said with a broad grin.

"Never you mind about that," Lucy said.

"No worries. I'm sure I'll be able to find it on my own," I said with my most saccharine smile.

Lucy was still giving Myra grief as I walked among the other offerings.

For a single moment in time, everyone seemed to vacate the small alcove where I was standing. It was as though they'd been moved out at the same time by some mysterious force, and it left me with an immediate sense of uneasiness.

Then I spotted Midnight, along with his new translucent friend. Silas might not still be around, but his daughter Summer was still there, apparently watching over her mother's things from beyond the grave.

"Is there anything I can do to help you?" I asked Summer

as I spotted the anguished expression on her face, feeling silly the second I heard my own words. She'd just died, after all. Summer looked as though she wanted to reply as Midnight nudged her with his nose, but they both vanished in an instant as an older man, quite alive, came around the corner and ruined our solitude. What had Summer been doing there, and how had Midnight managed to form a bond with her? Had he become some kind of guide to the afterlife when his own candle had been snuffed out? I hardly thought it could be a coincidence that the two of them were together, but stranger things had happened before in my life, including the reappearance of Midnight himself.

"Were you just talking to me?" the old man asked me.

"Sorry. I thought I saw someone that I used to know," I said feebly.

"Forgive me for saying so, but you look as though you've just seen a ghost."

"You don't know the half of it," I said as I made my way past him and headed outside.

By the time I left the house, my nerves had calmed down quite a bit. Either Summer would show up in my life again or she wouldn't, and there was nothing that I could do about it in the meantime. I wasn't entirely positive that she'd been trying to communicate with me, but I wasn't about to rule it out. Though the gossip around Noble Point believed that the farm deaths had been nothing more than a pair of tragic accidents, I was starting to become suspicious.

I had other things on my mind at the moment, though. Returning my attention to the auction, I decided that there were five boxes I wanted to bid on; I just hoped they went on sale before I had to leave. Strike that. If they weren't, I'd wait them out and open the shop whenever I got back, no matter how long that might take.

After looking around for a few minutes in vain, I finally found Lincoln relaxing in an old armchair that was painted a bright orange hue. He looked cool sitting in the shade cast from an ancient oak tree. "Hi, Christy. Would you care for a seat?" he asked as he gestured to the empty purple chair beside him.

"Where did you get these?" I asked as I sat.

"An enterprising young fellow is renting them out over there," Lincoln said as he pointed to a teenager with more business than he could handle at the moment.

As I looked around, I saw that Lincoln had found a perfect spot where we could see the auctioneer clearly but still be in the shade if the sun got too hot later. Late Spring brought on unpredictable changes in our climate, so there was no telling what kind of weather we'd be getting later.

"He's got quite a racket going, doesn't he?" I asked as I lightly stroked the chair's arms.

"I prefer to think of it as discovering the perfect niche market," Lincoln said. "He told me that he buys these chairs at every auction he goes to and ends up renting them out later. When he gets his new inventory home, he makes sure that they are sound, and then he paints them with distinctive colors so no one will try to walk away with them later."

"How did he get permission to do all of this from the auctioneer?" I asked.

"Are you kidding? He loves it. The more comfortable people are, the longer they'll stay, and the more they'll bid. It's absolutely brilliant."

"Did you find your pitchfork?" I asked. It really was quite thoughtful of Lincoln to rent the chairs for us, and I was glad again that I'd asked him to join me.

"It's there all right, but there's another buyer who wants it. The woman was practically drooling over it when I got there."

"Is *she* going to use it for hay?" I asked with a grin.

Lincoln's face clouded up a bit. If he noticed my smile, he didn't comment on it. "She wants to hang it on the wall as a *decoration*. I'm getting that thing, no matter how much it costs me."

"Seriously? Can you really afford to do that?" I knew that

I had limits with the purchases I could afford today, but I doubted that Lincoln had many such restraints. From what I'd heard around town, he was very good at what he did.

"Christy, I'm doing well enough to indulge myself every now and then, and this is something that I really want."

"When do you think that it's going to go up for bid?" I asked. "I heard someone say that the house's contents would go first, and then the tools in the barn would be last." I started to wonder if I might have to end up getting a ride back to the shop if Lincoln was held up waiting for his pitchfork to come up for bid.

"As a matter of fact, it's going up first," Lincoln said with a smug smile. "It cost me ten bucks to get it moved to the head of the line, but I know that we don't have all day."

"I should get you to do the same thing for the boxes that I'm interested in," I said, purely joking.

"I'd be delighted," Lincoln said with a smile. "What are the lot numbers?"

"I was just teasing you," I said.

"Nonsense. I'm having fun working the system."

I reluctantly handed over my list, and Lincoln took it before I could offer to pay him for the bribe.

He came back five minutes later, grinning broadly. "It's done."

"How much did it cost you this time?" I asked.

"Not a thing," Lincoln answered with a grin.

"How did you manage that?" This was something that I wanted to know.

"I approached the man bringing out the first lot and handed him your list. When he asked what it was all about, I told him that Mr. Johnson demanded that these be auctioned off first."

"Who's Mr. Johnson?" I asked.

"I have no idea, but it seems to have worked," Lincoln said, laughing mightily. "He was ready enough to do what I asked."

I joined him in laughter, happy that Lincoln was such good

company. The only thing putting a damper on the morning was Summer's sudden ghostly appearance, but since there was nothing I could do about that at the moment, I decided to make the best of the situation and try to enjoy myself.

I waited with anticipation to see what would be offered first, and sure enough, the first item up for bid was one of the boxes that I was interested in. It appeared that I'd even jumped to the head of the line in front of Lincoln's pitchfork.

As the auctioneer started his patter, I held up my number and called out a little too loudly, "Ten dollars."

"What are you doing, Christy? He only asked for a dollar for the opening bid," Lincoln whispered.

"What can I say? I got carried away." This wasn't an auspicious start, and I found myself hoping that someone else would outbid me so I could take a more rational approach with my next bid.

To my shock, no one else bid, though, and I won the first lot.

Even after overbidding, I still had the lion's share of my hundred-dollar auction budget left. Maybe this was the way to go after all.

I won the second, third, and fourth boxes as well with bids of ten dollars apiece again, but my luck ran out on the last box on my list. "Ten," I said again with more confidence this time.

"Twenty," I heard a woman say from just behind me. It was Lucy, and she was clearly unhappy that I'd been successful in acquiring so many of the boxes so far.

"Thirty," I said.

"Forty," Lucy countered immediately. She clearly hated being beaten earlier, and the woman was now trying to make up for it.

"Fifty," I said without giving it another thought. It wasn't about getting the last box of jewelry anymore. It was about winning.

"Isn't that a bit over your budget?" Lincoln asked me quietly. "You know, it won't be the end of the world if you don't get *everything* you had your eye on."

Maybe he was right. Perhaps I had overbid again. "I might have gotten a *little* carried away."

"Don't worry. I'll float you the rest, and you can pay me back later."

"No, I can manage just fine on my own." I wasn't sure what I'd do if Lucy tried to trump me again, though. My budget might have been stretched at that point, but I really didn't want to lose to Lucy. Then again, maybe it wouldn't be the worst thing in the world to lose out on the last box of trinkets.

"Are there any more bids?" the auctioneer called out. "Fair warning, this is your last and final call."

What was I thinking? It wasn't very businesslike of me to throw so much money at the last box, when I had the others already. I held my breath, hoping that Lucy would get in the spirit of things as well. After all, I had four boxes of trinkets already. Why did I feel the need to own the fifth?

"Sold," the auctioneer said as the gavel pounded down.

"Well done," Lincoln said.

"Thanks," I said, though I wasn't so sure. I started to get up to collect my boxes when Lincoln put a hand on my arm. "Hang on a second. My pitchfork is coming up next. Stay right where you are. I've got a hunch that you're going to bring me good luck."

"I'm not sure that it's true, but it's the least I can do after all you've done for me," I said as I settled back in my chair.

The auctioneer extolled the virtues of the old pitchfork, and I could see that Lincoln was tensing beside me. He really did want that memory from his past, and I hoped that he got it.

"Fifty dollars," he said after the auctioneer asked for ten to start. Lincoln winked at me. "I'm taking a play right out of your book."

"One hundred," a woman's voice from the back sang out.

"That's her," Lincoln told me as he glanced back into the crowd, and then he shouted out, "*Two* hundred."

There were several gasps from the crowd, and I was certain

that many of the folks present had no idea why Lincoln was bidding so strongly on something that had clearly seen better days.

"Two hundred fifty," the woman said a little tentatively.

"Don't give up now," I urged. "You've got her on the ropes."

"Three hundred," Lincoln said without a moment's hesitation, and then he added loudly over his shoulder, "Lady, bid as much as you want. I aim to get that pitchfork, and I can hang around here all day bidding you up."

There was laughter from some of the folks around us, and I could feel the group start to pull for him.

"We have three hundred. Do I hear four?" When there were no takers, he asked, "Three fifty? Anybody? First, second, last bid. Going, going," the auctioneer said, and his gavel hung in the air for what felt like hours before he finally slammed it down and said, "Gone. Sold for three hundred dollars."

The crowd applauded, and I added my own approval to the mix.

"Let's go collect our spoils," Lincoln said as he waved to the teen to tell him that we were finished with our chairs for the day.

"Do you regret spending so much on your pitchfork?" I asked him as we made our way to the table where we were supposed to pay.

"Not a chance. To be honest with you, it was worth ten times that to me," Lincoln said. "It's going in my office to remind me of where I came from. I want to look at it every day and remember what it was like to earn my living with my brawn instead of my brains."

"I'm glad that you got it, then," I said.

"How about you? You really cleaned up today."

"Let's just hope that I got some really good things to resell," I said.

"In all of that lot? You're bound to have picked up at least a few things the masses will love."

A man in the crowd called out in our direction, "Lincoln, do you have a second? I'm in some real trouble, and I need your legal advice."

"Come by the office, Harry. We can chat on Monday."

"This can't wait," he said. "I know it's not a good time, but if you'd talk to me for a minute or two, I'd consider it a personal favor."

"It's okay," I told Lincoln. "I'll go settle my bill. We've still got plenty of time before I have to open the shop, so we can meet up after you're finished."

"I don't really want to do that," Lincoln said with the hint of a frown. "It's *not* okay with me, Christy. This is supposed to be *our* time."

"It's really not a problem. There will be plenty of other chances for us to spend time together," I said.

"Do you promise?" Lincoln asked with a broad grin.

"Well, at least *one* more chance. Now go. I'll be fine."

"Okay. As annoying as Harry Baylor can be at times, he does have some deep pockets. I won't be too long."

A few minutes later, as I made my way through the crowd, I started reaching for my cash to pay at the auctioneer's table, but I got held up.

Someone stood in my way, and one look in Lucy's eyes told me that collecting my winnings wasn't going to be as easy as I'd hoped it would be.

Chapter 3

"I can't *believe* that you just *cheated* me," Lucy screamed at me. Fortunately, the auctioneer was getting excited about selling a sofa up on the makeshift stage, so most of Lucy's comments were drowned out by the quick patter of the man with the microphone.

"Exactly how did I cheat you, Lucy?" I asked, keeping my voice calm. "It was an auction. You were free to bid on anything you liked. It's not my fault that you didn't start until the last unit."

"Those boxes weren't supposed to be *first*," she protested in her shrill voice.

"But they were, weren't they? You can't complain about it to me. You had a chance to buy the last box. Why didn't you outbid me on that one?"

"Because I suddenly realized that it wasn't the one I wanted," she snarled. Lucy was close enough to me now that I could almost feel the heat radiating off of her.

"I'm sorry that you're angry, but it's not my fault."

"Listen," she said as she lowered her voice and took some of the edge out of it. "I get it. You found a way to beat me, fair and square. How about if I buy *everything* from you that you just bought? What did you pay altogether?"

"It doesn't matter," I said. "Those boxes are not for sale."

"Don't be that way, Christy. You're going to try to resell everything you got for a profit, so why not skip the middleman? I'm guessing that you paid about two hundred dollars for everything. Okay, I'll double your money. Four hundred dollars, right here and now. No muss, no fuss. What do you say?"

It was a fair offer for most folks, but I wasn't even tempted to take it. I had plans for that jewelry, and if things worked out in my favor, I could do a whole lot better than that in my store. "I appreciate your offer, but no thanks."

"Five hundred, then," Lucy said, her lips pursing into a frown. "Surely even *you* can't turn that down."

"I don't understand why you're suddenly so interested in what you called junk before," I said. Her enthusiasm was making me curious about her motivation. "After all, you said it yourself. It's just flashy costume jewelry."

"My reasons don't matter. I've made you an offer that's more than fair, and I expect an answer."

"Lucy, I'm sorry, but I can't take it. You're welcome to come by the shop later and see which pieces I put out on display, but the lot is going home with me."

"Okay, I'll tell you. My reasons are sentimental. Ginny and I were friends, but just before she died, we had a falling out. I've felt bad about it ever since, and getting back some of the things that I gave her might help ease my guilt. I'm begging you, Christy. Help me out here."

I was starting to feel bad about my hard stand. "I'll tell you what I'm willing to do. After I go through everything, I'll give you the first shot at buying a few things before I put them on sale for the general public. I'm sorry, but it's the best I can do."

"Forget it. That's not good enough. Mark my words. You're going to regret turning me down," Lucy said, any pretense of conciliation that she'd shown before now gone. "I'll make you pay for this, Christy."

"Is that a threat?" I asked. I'd meant to keep my voice down, but I'd failed miserably. "You should know something about me, Lucy. When I'm pushed, I push back."

"You're the one who doesn't have any idea who you're messing with," Lucy said, and then Myra was there by her side again.

"Lucy, keep your voice down! You're making a scene," Myra said.

"So what? She's goading me, and I won't have it."

"Remember what the doctor said about your heart. You mustn't allow yourself to get too upset, Lucy. It's not good for you."

Lucy took a deep breath, and then she nodded her reluctant agreement. "You're right. I was wrong to try and reason with her in the first place. Come on, let's go."

Myra looked pleased, and the two of them walked back into the crowd. I hadn't been around when Lucy and Ginny had supposedly been friends, but I thought about how I'd feel if Marybeth and I ever had a falling out, and I couldn't stand the thought. I meant what I'd said. I'd let Lucy have a look at what I was going to put on display if she still wanted to, but I didn't regret not selling the lot to her. I needed what I'd bought to keep my store fresh and ensure that my customers kept coming back.

I had just finished paying my bill when Lincoln joined me at the table where winning bids were redeemed. "What was that all about?" he asked as he handed over a check for the pitchfork that he'd bought earlier.

"What are you talking about?" I asked as I got my receipt.

"Don't even *try* to pretend that you don't know what I mean, Christy. I could hear you arguing with that woman over the auctioneer a few minutes ago, and that's saying something. His voice was even amplified."

"One of my customers was angry that I got the boxes she was interested in buying herself. Lucy must have been distracted by something, because she didn't realize that most of the merchandise that we were both interested in was up for sale until it was too late for her to bid on them."

"That's no reason for her to yell at *you*," Lincoln said. "Is there anything else that you're not telling me?"

"As a matter of fact, she offered me five times the money I spent if I'd sell her everything on the spot, but I turned her down."

Lincoln whistled softly. "That's a lot of money."

"I know that it might sound like it, but I should easily be able to make more than that selling the lot piecemeal at Memories and Dreams."

"That's a pretty healthy return on your investment,"

Lincoln said with a laugh.

"What can I say? Cora taught me to be a bargain shopper," I said, referring to my late boss. She'd been slain in the store, along with one of my cats, Midnight, and while I hadn't heard a whisper from Cora since the homicides, Midnight had made his presence known almost immediately. The recent appearance of Summer's ghost was a bit more startling, and I had to wonder if I'd seen the last of her.

"Cora did a fine job with your lessons, then," he said.

"Where would you like these?" a young man asked me as he showed up carrying the boxes I'd just purchased.

Lincoln said, "I didn't realize that these auctions supplied delivery services as well."

"We usually don't," the young man said with a grin, "but Mr. Hardacre was so impressed with how much you paid that he insisted I do this for you as a way of saying thank you for getting things rolling."

"That's great. Follow him, since we're going to *his* truck," I said as I pointed toward Lincoln.

"Christy, I'd be happy to carry your boxes myself, but this pitchfork would be a little awkward to balance with anything else," Lincoln said.

"That's okay. I'm happy to do it," the young man said. "I could use the break, actually."

"Then follow us," I said. "By the way, what's your name?"

"I'm Tommy Ambrose, ma'am."

"I'm not ma'am, not by a long shot. My name's Christy, and this is Lincoln."

"Nice to meet you both," Tommy said. "I'd shake hands, but they're full at the moment," he added with a grin.

As we started to walk toward Lincoln's truck, I bit my lower lip before I said, "With this kind of service, I've got a feeling that I paid too much for these boxes."

"Cheer up. At least one person believes that they're worth more," Lincoln said.

To my surprise, Tommy asked, "Are you two talking about that mean little woman who was just yelling at you, Christy?

I heard her friend call her Lucy before you showed up."

"How did *you* happen to run into her?" I asked.

"It wasn't a coincidence, if that's what you're asking," Tommy said. "She came over to where I was guarding your boxes and offered me a bribe to let her go through your things before you got there."

Why was I not surprised by Lucy's behavior? "Did she give you any idea what she was looking for in particular?" I asked.

"No, I never let it get that far. Fair is fair. You bought these boxes. They belonged to you."

"What did she say when you turned her offer down?" Lincoln asked with a grin.

Tommy returned the smile in kind. "All I can say is that she could teach lessons on swearing at the high school. I thought I'd heard everything, but she taught me some new words that I'm going to have to look up online before I trust myself to use them."

We got to Lincoln's truck, and Tommy slid the boxes onto the tailgate. "There you go."

I reached into my pocket for some money so I could tip him, but all I had was a single one-dollar bill. As I started to offer it to him, Tommy said, "Thanks, but like I said before, this was compliments of Mr. Hardacre."

"Be sure to thank him for me, then," I said. "It was nice meeting you, Tommy."

"You too, ma—Christy." He'd caught himself just in time.

Lincoln shook the young man's hand. "Thanks again, Tommy."

"You're very welcome."

As we drove back to town, Lincoln said, "We've still got quite a bit of time before you have to open your shop. Do you have any interest in doing anything else?"

"What did you have in mind?" I asked him.

"I don't know. We could drive around and chat if you'd like, or maybe go by Celeste's diner and get some coffee."

"As tempting as your offer sounds, what I'd really like to do is head back to Memories and Dreams and get started sorting through my treasures."

"Do you honestly think that you might have something valuable back there?" Lincoln asked as he gestured toward his truck bed.

"I'm not sure," I said. "I keep wondering why Lucy would put up such a fuss about those boxes unless there was something that the auctioneering company might not have known about. I don't buy her story about her friendship with Ginny going bad, so I keep wondering if there's something everyone else has missed."

"Let's find out, shall we?"

"Lincoln, are you sure you want to do that? It's not going to be very exciting; trust me."

"Come on, I've worked on puzzles with you before. You *know* that I can be helpful."

"I won't deny it. Let me ask you something. Do you think that it's possible that a real piece of jewelry is mixed in among all of the fakes?"

"I was wondering that myself, and to be honest with you, I'm dying to find out. It's settled then. We'll skip the coffee and go straight into sleuthing mode. I have one question, though. How are we going to know a real piece from a fake one if the auctioneers couldn't?"

"I know a little about authentic jewelry," I said, "and there are few basic tests I can try. If there's anything that I'm not sure about, I know somebody who might be able to help us."

"Then by all means, let's go back to Memories and Dreams and see what you've got."

We emptied the contents of all of the auction boxes by placing the items individually on a folding table that I kept in the back room. It was a large surface, one I kept on hand for the sidewalk sales I had every now and then, but at the moment it was covered with the gaudiest collection of costume jewelry I'd ever seen in my life.

"Should I go ahead and throw the wrapping paper and boxes away?" Lincoln asked.

"No, those are gold around here. Stack everything in the corner over there with the rest of my boxes. I use them all the time here at the shop, and the newspaper wrapping will come in handy, too."

"I like that. Never throw anything away."

"I don't if I might be able to use it later," I said. "Do me a favor, would you? Grab a few of those plastic storage bins on your way back over here, would you?"

Lincoln did as I'd asked and put them on a nearby chair. "These had to have cost you something."

"You might think so, but you'd be wrong. Cora got them at a salvage shop in Hickory," I said. "They were dirt cheap, and this way I can see what I've got after I sort through everything."

"Then we'll need to separate this stuff a little better than we have so far," Lincoln said. "Do you mind if I use that card table?"

"Do you mean my portable desk?" I asked with a grin. "Sure, why not?"

He put the tubs side by side and slid the lids under each storage bin. As Lincoln looked at the mounds of jewelry, he asked, "Where should we get started?"

"Just dig in and grab a piece."

"I'm afraid that I'm going to miss something valuable. What exactly am I looking for?" he asked.

"The first dead giveaway is the weight of the item. Anything that's made of real gold should have a heft to it. As for the jewels, it's not that hard to tell the fakes from the real thing, but if you're not sure, and I mean about anything, let me have a look before you put it in a bin. Oh, and take this."

I reached over and grabbed two small magnets. After I separated them, I handed one to Lincoln, and I kept the other one for myself.

"What am I supposed to use this for?" he asked.

"Gold and silver aren't magnetic," I said. "If a piece sticks to your magnet, it's not genuine."

"That's a cute trick," he said.

"It was another lesson from Cora," I replied.

"Is there anything else that I should know before we get started?"

"There are a few more things, actually," I said. "Besides the magnet test, we can use this," I said as I brought out an unglazed ceramic tile I'd bought for a dollar at our local hardware store. "We can rub a bit of any piece that we're not sure about to see if it's really gold."

"How will we be able to tell the difference between gold and something that's counterfeit?" Lincoln asked as he studied the tile.

"It sounds too simple to be true, but real gold leaves a gold streak, and fake gold leaves a black one."

"Fascinating," Lincoln said. "What else am I looking for?"

"I have a probe I use for diamonds, but I loaned it to a friend of mine who just got engaged, so we won't be able to use that right away. One good test is to fog the diamond as though it were a mirror. If the fog disappears quickly, there's a good chance that the stone is real. If it lingers, it's most likely a fake. I've also got a jeweler's loupe, but I'm guessing I won't need it."

"For the gold, couldn't we just check the markings? I thought they had to say what karat they were."

"There are a few problems with that," I said. "One, markings can wear off, especially on old jewelry, and two, what one man can make, another one can fake."

"So that's no good. Okay then, one more question before we get started. How can we tell if something is just gold plated, instead of being pure gold?"

"That's a very good question. One way is to look for worn edges. If another metal shows up underneath or you spot rust, then it's gold plated. The weight will help there as well. So, are you ready to get started?"

"I'm a little concerned that I'll make a mistake and get rid of something that's valuable," Lincoln said.

"Don't be. If there's any doubt in your mind, just ask me. Don't worry, Lincoln. Most of what we've got here is costume jewelry. I'm guessing that it won't be that hard to tell if we stumble across something genuine."

"Let's dig in then, shall we?"

As we started going through the pieces, it was quickly apparent that nothing of Ginny's was worth all that much. I'd be able to make a profit from it at the shop, but there were no home runs, at least not in the stuff that I bought.

"Hang on a second," Lincoln said as he held a ring up to the light. "I'm not sure, but I think that I might have something here."

"Let me take a look at it," I said as I took the ring from him. It was an old-fashioned engagement ring sporting a diamond that was rather nice. At least it would be if it turned out to be real. As I studied it, I said, "I must have missed this when I unloaded the boxes."

"I almost threw it over there in the pile of papers and boxes myself. It was wrapped up pretty tightly in a sheet of paper for some reason, almost as though someone didn't want this ring found."

"Why didn't they just steal it outright if they were just going to hide it?" I asked.

"Maybe there were too many people watching those boxes at the time. I don't know. I'm just glad that we found it instead of innocently throwing it away."

"I am, too. Let's see what we've got here." I fogged the diamond, and sure enough, the haze dissipated before I could even check it. That was a very good sign. Inside the band, the ring was too worn to show a stamp, but a gentle rub on the tile showed a gold streak.

"What do you know. We have a winner," I said.

"What do you think it's worth?" Lincoln asked, clearly caught up in the treasure hunt.

I took out my loupe and looked a little closer at the stone. "There are some small imperfections in the stone," I said after I studied the diamond a little closer.

"That's bad, isn't it?" Lincoln asked, clearly deflated by my news.

"On the contrary," I said with a smile. "It means that it's genuine."

"What do you think it's worth?" Lincoln asked.

"I'd say somewhere between two thousand to three thousand dollars," I answered. "That's an educated guess, but I'm still going to have Vera Covington take a look at it." Vera ran a fine jewelry store downtown, and she'd helped Cora out in the past. I had a hunch that she'd help me now.

"So, it's not really a fortune, is it?" Lincoln asked.

"Maybe not to you, but it's going to make my month pretty sweet," I said.

"Do you think that ring is why Lucy wanted the boxes that you bought?"

"I can't think of any other reason. The rest of this is clearly just costume jewelry," I said as I quickly examined what was left on the table. "I'll be able to make a tidy profit on it all in the shop, but the ring you found is the real discovery." I glanced at the clock and saw that we still had plenty of time before I had to open the shop. "I'd like to buy you lunch as a way of thanking you for all of your help, if you're interested."

"You bet I am," Lincoln said. "I just need to wash my hands first. This stuff was kind of nasty, wasn't it?"

"I'm not all that surprised. Nobody's cleaned any of it in years," I said as I tucked the diamond ring into my pocket. "Maybe we can stop by Vera's after we eat and see if she'll take a look at it."

"I'd love it. I won't even ask for a finder's fee," he said with a grin.

"What do you think lunch is all about?" I asked him, smiling in return.

"I figured that you just couldn't bear the thought of me leaving you so soon," he said.

I patted his arm. "Keep telling yourself that, Lincoln, and

someday you might believe it. If you wouldn't mind, let's move these bins up front so I can get started on building a display when I get back after lunch."

"That sounds like a plan to me," Lincoln said, and we quickly moved my latest finds up front where they'd be easier to dig through while I had customers in the shop.

"That takes care of that. Are you ready to go grab a bite to eat?" I asked.

"After you," he said.

I locked the shop back up, and we headed next door to Celeste's diner. After a quick bite there with Lincoln, I wanted to head straight to Vera's jewelry shop. I had a feeling that my estimate was pretty close, but it would be nice to get her verification of its worth. If she was interested in it, I wasn't sure if I should sell it directly to her or if I should try to sell it at the shop myself. There wasn't much call for engagement rings in Memories and Dreams, but then again, I was in no real hurry to move it. I'd have to wait and see what Vera thought of it, and then make my decision after that.

All I wanted at the moment was a nice lunch with Lincoln and a chance to enjoy myself now that the first part of the day's work was over. Opening the shop wouldn't be nearly as taxing as attending the auction had been. I wasn't sure if it was because of the stress of bidding or the fact that I'd seen Midnight's ghost with Summer, but the morning had taken a toll on me, and I was eager for things to get back to normal.

Whatever that meant.

Chapter 4

"Well, if it isn't the big auction winner herself," Celeste Montgomery said as Lincoln and I walked into her café next door to Memories and Dreams. Celeste was a lovely woman: thirty pounds overweight by modern standards, but it didn't dull her beauty by a single ounce. "I hear you really cleaned up out on Silas's farm today."

"How did you find out that fast?" I asked her. "We've only been back an hour."

"Lucy Brighton was in here a few minutes ago," Celeste said. "She's not too happy with you, but I wouldn't worry about it. Lucy's not happy about most things these days."

"What is her problem?" I asked her. "Things almost came to blows at the auction."

"I don't even know where to get started. So, did you find anything good?"

I considered telling her about the ring Lincoln had found, but I decided that it might be better if I kept that particular fact to myself. "It was about what I expected. I should do all right with it."

"Good. As long as you make a profit, that's all that counts, right?" Celeste asked. Turning to Lincoln, she said, "Counselor, it's been awhile since I've seen you in here for lunch."

"With my schedule lately, it's tough to get away from my desk, even on Saturdays."

Celeste wagged a finger at him. "It's not good to work yourself so hard."

Lincoln smiled at her. "Said the kettle to the pot. When was the last time *you* took a day off?"

"Let's see, what is this, Saturday? I'd say it's been almost eleven months."

"I rest my case," Lincoln said.

"Point taken. Feel free to sit anywhere you'd like. Two

sweet teas?"

"Please," Lincoln said.

"Actually, I'd like a glass of water, no lemon," I said.

"I'm sorry," Lincoln said as he turned to look at me. "I didn't mean to order for you."

"No worries," I said. "I'm just trying to cut back on my caffeine intake."

"You're giving up sweet tea?" Celeste asked in surprise.

"Not entirely. I'm just trying to trim it down a little. Don't worry. I can't imagine ever giving it up entirely."

Lincoln and I found a booth near one of the windows, and we sat down. "You're not going to hold that against me, are you?" he asked earnestly.

"What's that?" I asked as I looked at a menu.

"Ordering for you like that," he said.

"Relax," I said as I reached over and touched his hand lightly. "It's all good, okay?"

"Okay," Lincoln said with a smile.

At that moment, Celeste brought our drinks, and I pulled my hand away from Lincoln's quickly. The café owner smiled slightly, but at least she refrained from commenting. "Now then, what can I get for you both?"

Lincoln gestured to me, so I ordered first. "I'll have a club sandwich, no tomato and easy on the mayonnaise."

"Would you like fries with that?" she asked.

"Why not? After all, I'm not having tea."

"That sounds good to me, too," Lincoln said as he closed his own menu. "Only slap a tomato on mine, and use all the mayo you see fit."

"Will do," she said, and Celeste disappeared back into the kitchen to place our orders.

"How's life at the shop going overall?" Lincoln asked me after he took a healthy swallow of tea. I was beginning to regret not ordering some myself. Sure, I wanted to cut back on my caffeine, but was there any reason that I had to start right now?

"Christy, are you listening to me?"

"Sorry, but I've changed my mind."

"About having lunch with me?" he asked, clearly upset by the notion.

"No, of course not. I was talking about the sweet tea."

The relief flooded across his face. "We can remedy that easily enough." He got up, spoke with Celeste, and soon came back with another glass of tea. "Here you go."

"You didn't have to do that," I said.

"I know, but I wanted to."

I took a sip and savored the rich taste of the cold tea-and-sugar blend, taking it all in as though it were a fine wine. For me, it was better than *anything* alcoholic.

"You do like your sweet tea, don't you?" Lincoln asked.

"It's my major vice. I'll start cutting back tomorrow."

"That sounds like a solid plan to me. So, you didn't answer my question. How's life at the shop going?"

"It's good," I said. I'd been running Memories and Dreams for a while now, and I was finally starting to get used to the idea that in five years, the place would be mine. I was sure that Cora's relatives wouldn't be too pleased by the prospect, but that didn't factor into my decision to carry on my former boss's tradition. The only downside to my life at the moment was that Midnight's ghost was making fewer and fewer appearances, and I was afraid that his tie to me was slowly starting to fade. It would be bittersweet when he finally moved completely to the Other Side of life. On the one hand, I'd miss him terribly, but on the other, I hoped that he found new friends, fields filled with catnip, and all of the naptime he desired.

"Did I just sense a little hesitation in your voice as you said that?" Lincoln asked. He must have been really good in court, because he rarely missed a single nuance in our conversations.

"No, it's all quite lovely."

"But not what you signed up for when you graduated from college, I'll wager. This all kind of fell into your lap, didn't it? You came to visit Marybeth, but you ended up staying."

"Life is kind of like that, isn't it?" I asked as I took another sip of the delicious tea. "My favorite expression has always been, 'Man plans, and God laughs.' It's been the story of my life."

"Well, at least it keeps things interesting."

"Sometimes in a Chinese curse kind of way," I said.

"May you live in interesting times. Yeah, I like that one, too."

Our sandwiches and fries arrived, and we had a pleasant conversation as we ate. Lincoln made me laugh a few times, something I cherished after so much sadness in my life recently.

When the check arrived, we both reached for it.

"This is my treat, remember?" I reminded him.

"I'm not sure that we ever fully established that," he answered.

"Let me put it this way. If you want the opportunity to ever return the favor," I said with a smile, "you'll let me take care of this one. It's my way of thanking you for today."

"By all means, then. You pay. Thanks for lunch. Do you have any interest in having dinner with me so I can take my turn?"

"Tonight?" I asked.

"Why not? Sooner is almost always better than later."

I laughed. "I admire your persistence, but let's slow down a little, okay?"

"Hey, you can't blame a guy for trying," he said with a smile.

"I don't. As much as I appreciate the offer, let's do it some other time."

"You don't mind if I keep asking you out, then?" he asked.

"To be honest with you, I'll be kind of hurt if you don't," I said.

I paid the check and left Celeste a nice tip. As we walked out of the diner, I said, "I know you're busy, so you don't have to go to the jeweler's with me if you don't have time."

"Are you kidding? I'm dying to find out what that ring is

worth myself," Lincoln said. "If you don't mind, I'd love to go with you."

"Let's go see what we found, then."

"It's nice," Vera Covington said after she examined the ring I'd recently acquired. Vera was dressed in a spectacular black outfit, and her hair and nails were done to perfection. Vera's jewelry shop offered the best that Noble Point had, and I didn't normally let myself be tempted by even window-shopping there.

"Nice, but not great, right?" I asked.

"I hate to disappoint you, but it's actually rather pedestrian."

"What would you say that it was worth?" I asked.

"Full retail value? I'd mark it as nineteen ninety nine if I were selling it in my estate jewelry section."

"What would you take for it, though?" I asked her with a grin.

Vera smiled in return. The shop was empty at the moment, so her candor wouldn't cost her anything. "Bottom line? I'd take fifteen hundred. It's probably worth twelve, and I'd pay a grand for it."

"Those are nice margins," Lincoln said with a whistle.

Vera didn't take offense. "Look around you, Counselor. All of this splendor comes at a price."

"I don't doubt for one second that it's worth every penny," Lincoln said with a smile.

"Is that what you're offering me, a thousand dollars?" I asked.

"I might be able to go up to eleven, since it's you," Vera answered. "I'd like to keep my relationship with Memories and Dreams. Cora was a dear friend of mine, and I sincerely hope that we develop that ourselves."

"So do I," I said. "It's a deal. I'm not beating you up too badly, am I?"

"Not at all. Just realize that I might not be quite so generous in the future."

"Hey, I can always turn down any offer you make, can't I?" I asked with a smile.

"Isn't it wonderful having options?" she asked as she moved to her register. After Vera rang up a No Sale, she counted out eleven hundred dollars and handed me the cash, along with a receipt. "Christy, it's a pleasure doing business with you."

"You, too," I said as I folded the money in half and tucked it into my jeans.

"You wouldn't care to do a little shopping while you're here, would you?" Vera asked with a slight smile.

"No, thanks. No offense, but my speed is more along the lines of costume jewelry."

Vera laughed as she waved a hand in the air. "To each her own. It was nice seeing you both. I didn't realize that you were a couple."

"We're not," I said before Lincoln could say a word. "Not that I wouldn't…it's just that…you know, it's complicated."

"I'm so sorry that I asked," Vera said.

"It's fine," I said weakly as Lincoln and I left her shop.

Out on the sidewalk, I immediately turned to Lincoln. "I didn't mean anything by that, so don't read anything into what I just said. Vera just caught me off guard."

"It's fine," Lincoln said, though I could detect a hurt edge in his voice.

"No, it's clearly not. I don't know what just got into me." I frowned, and then I stepped closer to him and kissed him lightly on the lips.

"What was that for?" Lincoln asked, clearly confused by my impulsive gesture as I quickly stepped backward.

"I don't know. I just thought…sometimes I can be a real mess. I'm sorry."

"I'm not," Lincoln answered with a fresh smile. "Christy, feel free to kiss me anytime."

"I need to get inside my shop and lock the door behind me before I make an even bigger fool of myself than I already have," I said. I could feel my cheeks growing warm. Was I blushing? Oh my word.

"I'll see you later," Lincoln said as he took off on foot in the opposite direction toward his law office. If he skipped even once, I was going to kill him. "I'll pick my truck up later."

I headed back to Memories and Dreams, but as I glanced over at Vera's jewelry shop, I saw that she was standing in the doorway with a broad grin on her face.

I threw a hand up to wave good-bye, and then I walked down the street, wondering who else had seen me kissing Lincoln on the street in broad daylight.

As I walked up to the shop, I heard a noise coming from the alley behind Memories and Dreams. At first I thought it might just be my imagination, but when I heard it again, I decided to investigate. I could have called the police, but I didn't want to bother Sheriff Kent. It was probably nothing, but just in case, I picked up a short piece of two-by-four I found on the ground to use as a weapon if I needed to defend myself.

As I took another step forward, I heard something else.

My hands were shaking as I walked deeper into the alleyway.

"I've got a weapon," I said loudly, hoping that my voice didn't shake. "Come out with your hands up, and nobody has to get hurt." It sounded silly to me even as I said it. What did I think I was doing, acting on a bad television show?

"Don't shoot," I heard a woman's voice. "I'm not armed."

I took the final step around the corner and found Lucy Brighton standing hip-deep in my garbage.

"Lucy, what are you doing?"

"I tried knocking on the door, but you didn't answer," Lucy said.

"I was at lunch. That still doesn't explain why you're digging through my trash."

"Would you put that board down?" she asked. "I'm no

threat to you."

I'd honestly forgotten that I was even holding it. I lowered it, but I still held onto it. Somehow, it gave me comfort having it in my hands. "So, what exactly are you doing?"

"I lost one of my earrings at the auction," she said as she put her thumb behind one naked lobe. "I figured it must have fallen into one of the boxes you bought, so I was hoping to find it here. Have you already unpacked them?"

I decided not to answer that just yet. "What does your earring look like?"

Lucy stepped closer, and I saw a single dangling silver earring that was quite distinctive.

"I didn't find it anywhere in the things that I just bought," I replied.

"So, you've already unpacked," she said. Was there a hint of wistfulness in her voice, or was it just my imagination?

"I have. Sorry I couldn't help."

"Maybe you just missed it. There were a great many pieces in those boxes. My earring could have fallen into one of the boxes or the wrapping paper, and you might not have even seen it. I'd like to look through it all, if you don't mind, but I can't find any of those boxes back here."

"I don't generally throw good boxes away in my business," I said. And that's when it hit me. She wasn't looking for an earring at all. Lucy was most likely hoping that I'd missed the one ring of value in all of the boxes I'd just purchased. I had thought that it was odd when Lincoln discovered the diamond engagement ring wrapped tightly in paper. If I had to guess, Lucy had hidden it there herself, hoping that it had gone unnoticed. She couldn't steal it outright, since there was a chance that someone at the auction might catch her in the act.

"Then let me see them for myself," she said.

"I'm sorry, but I can't do that," I replied. "I've gone through them thoroughly. As a matter of fact, I found a diamond engagement ring in one of them that would have been easy to miss if I hadn't been careful." There was no reason to tell her that Lincoln had found it. The point that counted was that it had already been discovered.

Lucy shrugged. "It's probably not even real, but I'd be interested in buying it from you. I just so happen to *like* fake engagement rings."

It was clearly all a tissue of lies. "Sorry. I've already sold it, and for your information, it was real enough."

"You were *supposed* to give me the first opportunity to buy whatever you found, remember?" Lucy asked, clearly agitated.

"I promised you a crack at the costume jewelry," I reminded her. "I never said anything about the real pieces. If you'd like to come in with me, I have them sorted now."

"That can wait, but I happen to need a few boxes and some paper for wrapping. I'm sending my sister some things in California. I'll give you a few bucks for the boxes from the auction."

"I've already got plans for them," I said, though that wasn't the truth at all. There was just something about Lucy that put me on edge, and I didn't want her going through my back room, let alone be by myself with her. "Fair warning. I'm going to build a new display with some of the pieces I just bought, so this is your last chance to look at them."

"Fine, I'll look now," she said, the exasperation clear in her voice.

"Don't do me any favors," I said. I'd just about had my fill of her.

"No, you're right. You were nice enough to offer. I'm sorry for the way I've been behaving. I'm just under a little stress right now."

That didn't excuse her actions earlier, but I didn't have to be so hard on her, either. "What's going on? Is there anything I can do to help?"

"No, I'm beyond help at this point," Lucy said as she choked back a tear.

What was going on with this woman? Did she need to be on some kind of medication? It wasn't exactly a question I could ask, but I had to wonder. "Let's go see if we can find you something pretty," I said as I dropped the wood and walked to the front of the shop.

I glanced back to see if she was following me, and that's when I saw Lucy hesitate beside the two-by-four I'd just discarded. Had she honestly been about to pick it up and use it on me? When she looked up and saw that I was watching her, she smiled at me and kept walking, and I had to believe that it was all in my imagination. I was getting way too paranoid for my own good.

After I let Lucy in the door, I hesitated before I flipped the CLOSED sign to OPEN and found myself hoping for a customer to keep us company. After all, it didn't make any sense not to be careful. At least Lincoln and I had moved the bins up front before we'd gone to lunch. That kept Lucy and me out in the open where anyone passing by could glance in the window. The storeroom in back was just a little too isolated for my taste.

"Help yourself," I said as I pointed to the plastic bins.

"What are *you* going to be doing?" she asked me.

"I'm going to be going through them with you, of course," I replied. "I'm building a display around them, so I can sort through each bin after you're done with it."

Lucy looked disappointed that I'd be staying with her the entire time. It was clear that her heart wasn't in it as she looked through the items I'd just bought. After a few minutes, she pushed the last bin away. "There's nothing here that I want after all."

"That's surprising, since you were willing to pay me so much just a few hours ago."

Lucy tried to laugh. "What can I say? You saved me a lot of money this morning. I'm going to take off now."

"I'll keep an eye out for your earring," I said casually.

For a second, it seemed as though she'd forgotten all about her earlier excuse for digging through my trash. "Yes, I'd appreciate that," she said a little too late to be convincing.

After Lucy was gone, I decided that I'd had enough of

people for a while. Even if it meant missing out on a few sales, I flipped the sign back to CLOSED and started arranging some of the prettier pieces on the counter for sale. It was difficult to showcase the costume jewelry to their best advantage. As I started to play with the gaudy pieces, I realized that what I really needed was some black felt, or some kind of material to display them on to show them off to their greatest advantage. Cora had been a master at displaying items to make them look their best, but it was something I was just getting the hang of myself.

It only took thirty seconds for me to abandon any plans for a new display, though.

Midnight and her new friend, Summer, were both suddenly in front of me, in all of their translucent glory.

It appeared that my shop had just come down with ghosts.

Chapter 5

"Summer, what's going on? Why are you here?" I asked. I had no idea if she could talk to me at all, or even see me, for that matter. I had worked out the basics of communicating with Midnight when he'd first reappeared, so I knew that ghosts could generate sounds. Well, at least my cat could. But I'd never tried to talk to the ghost of a person before.

Apparently that all was about to change.

"You can really *see* me, Christy?" the ghost woman asked as she stared at me. "How is that even possible?"

"I don't really know, but I can hear you, too. All I can say for sure is that you're in my shop, and my cat, Midnight, is right beside you."

"Mrerewer," Midnight said, as though what I'd just said was too obvious to merit an intelligent comment. He was like that, never afraid to put me in my place if my actions and comments failed to live up to his expectations.

"But that's incredible. I haven't been able to make the slightest impression on anyone else, and I'd just about given up trying when your cat found me. Did you say that his name was Midnight?"

"It is. When I got him, he was as dark as a moonless night, so it seemed appropriate. My other cat is named Shadow, since he seems to constantly live around the edges."

"Is he a ghost, too?" Summer asked.

"No, he's still on my side of the Great Divide. I'm glad that you and Midnight found each other." I paused a moment, and then I added, "That must be it."

"What's that?"

"Midnight is probably acting like some kind of bridge between us. I certainly haven't seen any other ghosts since he first appeared to me." I had something delicate I wanted to bring up, but I wasn't sure how to go about it. Ghosts had feelings too, or at least I was going to assume they did until I learned otherwise. After all, Midnight had already shown me a variety of emotions and attitudes, so why should people be any different? "Have you seen your father since it happened? He's not here, is he?" I asked as I looked around the sales floor. That was all that I needed at the moment, another ghost in my life.

"No, my dad Moved On the moment it happened. If I had to guess, I'd say that he left the moment he could because he wanted to be with Mom. Their faith was something to see. The two of them were inseparable in life, and I lived in constant fear that he'd do something to hasten his own death in order to be with her."

"But you decided to stay behind," I said as my voice trailed off into nothingness.

"I couldn't let whoever did this get away with it," Summer said. "Don't get me wrong. The pull to Move On is pretty strong, but I'm fighting it with everything I've got."

"What *did* happen that night at the farm? It wasn't an accident, was it?"

"That's what's so frustrating," Summer said. "The last day of my life is clouded and blurry. I try to reach back for the memories, but it's almost as though they've been blocked from me. I wonder if it's like that for everyone once they get to the Other Side."

"I don't have a clue," I said. "You're my first experience with a *human* ghost." Was that what was keeping Midnight on This Side? Was he too much a part of my life to let his old ways go and embrace the new? It nearly made me cry when I thought of it that way. "Can you touch him?" I asked softly as I looked down at Midnight's shimmering image.

"No," she said with a hint of exasperation in her voice. "It took me a while to corner him before I could even try. I've got a hunch that he wasn't all that overtly affectionate when he was alive. Am I right?"

"I don't know if I'd say that, but he did take awhile to warm up to strangers," I agreed.

"Well, I tried to stroke his back, but my hand went right

through him."

That was new information, and valuable to have. So far, I'd learned that ghosts couldn't touch each other, and their memories were blocked for what had to be the most traumatic time of their lives. The knowledge gave me a little comfort. Most likely Midnight didn't remember the act that had killed him, and neither did Cora. I wasn't sure where my former boss and friend was now, but I was certain that she'd taken the opportunity to Move On to the next plane without a single look back. Cora had always been ready for what was next in life, and there was no reason to believe that she'd treated death any differently.

"That's okay. I'm sure Midnight appreciates the intention, if not the deed. Summer, is there any reason to believe that someone might have wanted to kill you and your father?"

"It's hard to imagine, but I know in my heart that what happened to us was no accident. It's a despairing moment when you start thinking about the folks who wouldn't mind seeing you dead."

"Why would anyone want to kill you *or* your father?" I asked.

"I have a few ideas, but nothing that's really solid. Christy, do you have any idea how I might be able to find out?"

"We'll get to that in a moment, but I have one more question for you. I hate to bring this up, but is there any chance that what happened to your mother was foul play as well?"

"Nobody killed my mom," Summer said, and she sounded dead certain of the fact.

It was clear that particular topic was off-limits, so I decided to drop it, at least for now. "But you're sure that the same doesn't go for you or your dad. If I'm going to help, I'll need that list of your suspicions."

A spark of light flashed in Summer's eyes, and for just a moment, she transformed into a nearly solid presence, though the manifestation only lasted a moment. "Do you mean that? You'll really help me uncover who killed my father and me?"

I grinned as I glanced over at Midnight, who looked smug about my declaration. "I really don't have much choice. Midnight has clearly set his mind to it, and there's nothing I can do to change it. Believe me, I've tried often enough in the past."

"Thanks, Midnight," Summer said as she looked over at him, and I could swear that crazy ghost cat of mine nodded his acknowledgment in her direction.

"So, where should we begin?" I asked.

"I wish I knew," she said, and it appeared as though the ghostly woman was on the verge of tears. I hadn't even imagined that ghosts could cry, but I had a hunch that I was about to find out if I didn't do something, and fast.

"Let's try this from a different angle. Most of the folks who are murdered know the people who killed them."

"That's kind of a grim thought, isn't it?" she asked.

"There's something that's even worse than that. You'd be amazed by how many folks are actually murdered by a family member."

Summer frowned, and in her anger, she again became a little more solid for a moment. Was that why poltergeists could move things around? Maybe they were just spirits who were angry all of the time, and who could blame them? I didn't fancy being dead any more than they must have. "Christy, I absolutely did *not* kill my father."

"I never thought for one moment that you did," I said quickly. "Let's find out who might have though, shall we? Tell me anyone who had a cross word with you or your dad recently, and anyone who might have been nursing a grudge against either one of you, no matter how small it might seem to you right now."

Summer nodded solemnly as she pointed to a pad of paper and a pen beside the register. "It might not be a bad idea if you take notes," she said.

"I'm ready whenever you are," I said as I retrieved the materials and prepared myself to start my unofficial investigation into the deaths of Summer and her father.

"The first person you need to speak with is Stick."

"Stick Oakhurst?" I asked.

"Do you know anybody else around here named Stick?" she asked me with a smile.

"The man must weigh three hundred pounds," I said. "Was he *ever* skinny?"

"Not that I can imagine," Summer said. "From what Dad used to say, Stick has always been on the large and round side. Calling him Stick was as clever as his friends ever got, and the name stuck."

"Why would Stick want to see you dead?" I asked.

"I'm not really sure. All I know is that he was on the farm a week before all of this happened, and it wasn't pretty. I had dinner with Sandy North and Helen Blankenship, my two best friends from high school. Dinner broke up early because Sandy's babysitter got sick, and since her husband walked out on her, she's raising the kids alone. Helen left, too, so I decided to make it an early night myself. As I walked up onto the porch, I heard Stick and Dad inside the house arguing about something."

"Did you happen to overhear what it was about?" This could be my first real clue.

"They both sounded as though they'd been drinking, something my father had been doing more and more of lately. Stick said that if Dad wouldn't share, he'd just take half of it himself."

"Share what?"

"I have no idea. Dad was about to say something when I took a step forward to hear better when I hit those blasted wind chimes Mom made him put up on the porch. They both came outside, and I pretended that I'd just driven up. I wasn't the only one acting, though. Stick and Dad appeared to be best buddies, but I'd heard them earlier, and there was no way that I could have been mistaken. Something was very wrong between them."

"What could it have been?" I asked. "I kind of think of Stick as being a happy, dim kind of guy. Was he really threatening your father?"

"There was no doubt in my mind about it. I asked Dad about it in a roundabout way the next day, but I couldn't get a word out of him. Something was going on there, though."

"I'll talk to Stick soon. Maybe I can get something out of him."

"Good luck," Summer said. "I sure didn't have any trying to learn anything from my dad."

"Maybe you were too close to the situation," I said. "Is there anybody else I should look at?"

Summer looked miserable, but I was happy to see that she was ready to keep answering my questions. "I don't know what happened at the auction, but I have to wonder about who ended up buying the place, and who bid for it and lost," she said sadly. It didn't surprise me that losing her family home was a major blow, though clearly not as much as being murdered had been. "Doesn't it make sense that *they'd* be suspects? After all, the only thing they'd be sure to get out of our deaths would be the opportunity to buy our family farm."

"Is it really all that valuable?" I asked. "If it was, why would your cousin sell the place so quickly?" I'd heard that Summer's cousin, Jan Billings, had been the sole person to inherit. "Hey, do you think that there's a chance that *she's* the one who killed you both?"

"I can't even bring myself to consider it," Summer said. "Jan and I were never really that close, but she has money of her own. She wouldn't have to murder us to get it."

"What makes you think that she has money?"

Summer frowned, an odd sight to see while looking at a ghost. "I don't know. I guess I've just always assumed that it was true. She's *always* had cash on her. Uncle Lee left her a fortune when he died."

"A lot of people seem to have died who were close to her," I said. "I don't mean any offense, but she needs to go on the list as well."

"I find that I'm far less concerned with what the living think about me now that I'm dead," Summer said. "But I think Jan is going to be a dead end."

"Maybe so, but I'm still going to put her on my list."

"You're right; you might as well include her, too. She lives in Tryon's Gap."

"That's less than half an hour away," I said.

"It's even closer to the farm," Summer said. "But I still think you're wasting your time."

"That's okay. I don't mind. Is there anyone else?"

She appeared to think about it, and then Summer said, "Not that I can think of right off the top of my head. It's not really much help, is it?"

"Don't kid yourself. You've given me a good start," I said. I glanced at my notes, and when I looked back up, I saw that Summer was beginning to flicker on and off. "Are you okay?"

She shrugged, and I worried about her, regardless of her current state. "Sorry. I'm doing the best I can. Christy, this is really *hard*."

"I know that it can't be easy making a list of folks who might have killed you," I said.

"It's not that, though it's true that part of it is difficult, too. I'm talking about staying here with you and talking. It's a real chore to make myself heard."

I looked around the room, and I suddenly realized that I couldn't see Midnight. "How are you even managing to stay without Midnight's presence nearby?"

"I'm not," Summer said with a smile as she pointed to the top of one of the display cases. Midnight was nearly impossible to see from his post, but a flicker of his ghostly tail showed me that he was still there. "For some reason, I *know* that I can't do it without him," Summer said.

"We should wrap this up for now," I said as I looked down at my jumble of notes. "I've been wondering about something. Where do you go when you're not here?"

"I can't tell you," she said solemnly.

"Is it some kind of rule?" I asked as I lowered my voice.

"No; if there are any rules, no one has told them to me yet.

I just meant that I'm here, and then I'm not. I don't know where I am in between. Does that make any sense at all?"

"It will have to do, won't it?" I asked. In a way, Summer's answer was more troubling than I'd expected. Did Midnight just cease to exist when he wasn't nearby? It was too horrible a thing to even think about.

"I'll let you go in a second," I said as I ciphered out part of one of my notes. "I just need to know—"

"Christy, are you talking to yourself again?" Lincoln asked as he walked in through the front door.

I didn't even have to look around to know that Summer and Midnight were both already gone. If I was going to continue to have conversations with ghosts, I was going to have to remember to lock that door.

"Lincoln, what are you doing here? Don't tell me that you missed me already."

"I'm trying to woo you, not stalk you and scare you away permanently," he said with a grin. "I was going to run a few errands, so I came back here to collect my transportation. When I got in the front seat though, I found something you might need. You forgot this in my truck." He held up my checkbook and waved it in the air. "I thought you might miss it."

"I don't write that many checks anymore since I got my debit card, but yeah, it might come in handy," I said as I took it from him. "Are you finished for the day?"

"I'd hoped to be, but Harry Baylor said that he really needed my advice at the auction, so I promised to squeeze him in. I shouldn't be too long, though. What are you going to do after you close up for the day?"

I was going to do some sleuthing, as a matter of fact, but I wasn't sure that I wanted to admit that to Lincoln. "I have a few things going on," I said.

"Well, if there's any room in your schedule, be sure to pencil me in."

"What did you have in mind?" I asked.

He just laughed. "Now where's the fun in me telling you

now?"

"Then we'll play it by ear," I said.

"That's fine. You've got my number."

I smiled at him. "Is that part of your wooing strategy, to keep me on my toes?"

"If it is, it wouldn't be to my benefit to tell you, would it?"

After he was gone, I called out tentatively into the empty shop. "Summer? Are you there? Midnight? Hello?"

No ghosts appeared at my summons, so I decided that until they came back, I'd have to do the best I could with what I had. The notes could be helpful, but before I could start looking for a murderer, I had to confirm that a double homicide had even taken place, if I could manage it.

It was time to call Sheriff Kent and see if he could shed a little light on the actual cause of the deaths for me. I just hoped that no customers came into the shop during my telephone call, an odd wish for any merchant to make, but I needed privacy to ask the kind of questions I was about to pose, and the last thing I needed was anyone else listening in on my end of the conversation.

"Sheriff, this is Christy Blake. Do you have a second?"

"I've been trying to track down some moonshiners, but I just lost their trail. What happened, Christy? Did you catch another shoplifter in your store?"

I'd caught an older man stealing a pocket watch on display the week before, and I'd managed to entice him with an antique chain in back while I called the sheriff. The man had folded quickly enough when the sheriff had come by, and it turned out that he was a habitual thief, but only of various timepieces. The last time he'd been arrested, he was trying to extricate a grandfather clock out of the back of a jewelry store by himself, and according to the report, he'd nearly given himself a hernia in the attempt.

"No thieves today, at least not that I'm aware of. I'm calling you about the official causes of death for Summer and Silas Bentley."

"It was an accident, plain and simple," the sheriff said with a hint of ire in his voice. "The coroner declared it after finding a heater on-site that was faulty. Carbon monoxide is known as a silent killer for a reason, Christy."

"Is there *any* chance that it was foul play?" I asked.

"I suppose there's a chance, but it's highly unlikely," Sheriff Kent said. "Why? What have you heard?"

"You know this town better than I do," I said. "There are rumors flying all over the place about what *really* happened to them." That wasn't true, at least as far as I knew, but I had a hunch that the cover story would be easy enough for the sheriff to believe.

"Folks around here have too much time on their hands and not enough to do with it," he said.

"So, you don't think it was murder?"

"Christy, I swear that if you weren't my favorite niece's best friend, I'd lock you up just out of spite. You wouldn't happen to be spreading those rumors yourself, would you?"

"I haven't said a word about it to a living soul," I said, proud of myself for strictly adhering to the truth.

That seemed to mollify him a little. "Well, see that you don't. I get the fact that we'd all like to find reasons for the things that happen to folks that we know and care about, but sometimes when people die, there's no sinister cause behind it. Accidents happen, and that's exactly what killed the two of them. Silas stacked a bale of hay too close to the exhaust pipe, and the shutoff on the heater never tripped. The combination shouldn't have happened, but it did. Don't look for anything sinister about it."

"How do you know that someone didn't move that hay bale there themselves and rigged the switch while they were at it?" I asked.

"Because that would make it murder, and nobody killed the two of them. Is that all you want?"

"I was just wondering about it, since I picked a few things at the auction," I said. "I couldn't hang around to see how it all turned out. Who ended up with the farm? Do you happen to know?"

The sheriff said, "I made it out there just in time to see Jack Baron and Bud Lake going at it tooth and nail. If you ask me, pride got in the way of good sense. Bud clearly wanted the place, but Jack wasn't about to let him have it. In the end, he had the deepest pockets, so he won the final bid."

"Do you really think that he paid too much for the farm?"

"Everybody does," Sheriff Kent said. "If I were Bud Lake, I'd buy Jack Baron dinner for saving him from making a colossal mistake, but I doubt that it's going to happen in my lifetime. Anything else?"

"That's it. Thanks for the information."

"You're welcome. Give my niece a hug for me when you get home, would you?"

"How do you know that I'm not there right now?" I asked.

"I just drove by your shop, and I saw that you were still open for business. Talk to you later, Christy."

"Bye," I said, and then I hung up the telephone. I'd learned quite a bit in the past hour, but there was still a wealth of information that I didn't have yet. If I was going to solve the double murder, I was going to have to do some real digging into what had really happened to Summer and Silas. I had a hunch that the sheriff and the coroner had both wanted the simplest explanation to be true, that the two had been killed by an accident, but Summer's presence, as well as her suspicions, made me believe that there was more to the story than that.

In the meantime, though, I had a shop to run, and I couldn't afford to lock my doors and turn away any potential sales. Cora had taught me early on that little sales often added up to become big ones, and you could never tell who was going to spend a lot of cash based on how they were dressed, or even the way that they acted.

I needed some income, and I'd just expanded my inventory in the hopes that it might help. To increase my foot traffic, I decided to take my sidewalk sign and make up a new teaser. After a few minutes, I wrote, "Brand New Stock! Jewelry!

Jewelry! Jewelry!" I thought the exclamation marks gave it a particularly urgent feel. It wasn't exactly Shakespeare, but then again, that wasn't what was required. All I wanted to do was to get some warm bodies inside the shop.

After that, my inventory would have to do the trick.

Chapter 6

Ten minutes later, I had my first legitimate customer of the day.

A harried man in his mid-forties dressed in a threadbare suit came into the shop, and after a few minutes of searching, he asked me, "Where do you keep your cows?"

"Excuse me?"

"Cows. Bovines. Those things that go moo. You know, cows."

"I'm sorry, but we're not a farm. You do realize that, don't you?"

He grinned at me. "My daughter has an obsession with cows, all kinds, shapes, sizes, and forms. Surely in this impressive store of yours you have at least one cow."

I thought about it for a few seconds, trying to come up with anything cow-related in our inventory. "How old is your daughter?"

"She's going to be twelve tomorrow," he said.

"Does she have pierced ears yet?"

He thought about it, and then he shook his head. "I have no idea. Her mother is in charge of that stuff, and I only get to see Emma every other weekend. Why do you ask?"

"I have a set of cow earrings, but they are for pierced ears," I said as I showed him the earrings in question. They were quirky, and I was surprised that no one had grabbed them yet.

"Do you have anything else?" he asked.

"Hang on. We have a cast-iron cow, but he has wings. Would that do?"

"How big is it?" he asked. "I don't have my truck with me today."

"It's nowhere near that big. In fact, it will fit in the palm of your hand," I said.

"It sounds perfect. Let's see it."

I walked over to our section filled with odd little things that defied any of our regular categories and picked up the cow. "Here you go."

"Wow. It's heavy," he said as he took it from me. "Are you sure that it's not lead?"

"I'm positive. It's two cast-iron pieces bolted together."

"Why wings, do you suppose?" he asked as he studied it.

"I like to think of them as angel wings," I said.

He got it immediately, something that pleased me immensely. "Holy cow."

"Exactly."

"I'll take it. Do you gift wrap?"

"Not normally, but for you, I'll make an exception."

"Perfect," he said.

"I'll be right back." I went into the back and got a box for the cow, along with some bubble wrap and some generic birthday wrapping paper Cora had picked up on sale. Carrying it all back out front, I found the man waiting for me by the front desk.

"This is awkward," he said when I rejoined him.

"Did you change your mind?"

"No, but I forgot to ask how much it was," he said. That explained him shopping in my eclectic used store for his daughter's birthday present. I'd hate to disappoint him, or his daughter, especially since the cow was going to be going to such a good home.

"This is your lucky day. It's five dollars, and that includes the wrapping," I said. The cow had come in a box filled with other trinkets, and I'd already made a healthy profit from the other things that had been included, so I could afford to give him a good price on it.

"Five dollars would be outstanding," he said with a grin. He counted out five wrinkled ones and laid them on the counter. "She's going to love it."

"I'm glad," I said. As I handed the wrapped present to him, I said, "Wish your daughter a happy birthday from me, would you?"

"I'd be happy to. Thanks again," he said as he waved the

box in the air on his way out of the shop. I could have probably gotten twice what I'd charged him for the cow, but one of the reasons I loved Memories and Dreams so much was that I could help make some people's lives just a little better. I knew that I wasn't curing diseases or saving lives, but I figured that adding a few extra smiles to the world every now and then was a pretty noble calling, too.

It was nearing my usual closing time, and I'd only had a few customers come in after my cow buyer, so I decided to close the shop early and do some snooping. I'd made up a solid list after speaking with Summer, so it wasn't like I didn't have anywhere to start looking. As a matter of fact, I had too many suspects on my list. It was time to get out and start narrowing it down, so I pulled in my sign and got ready to shut down for the day. With the front door locked, I kept expecting Midnight and Summer to show up, but evidently they'd both expended too much energy earlier to make a return visit so soon. I hoped that Midnight wasn't burning out faster because of his mission to help Summer, but if he was, it was for a good cause. A lot of people think that cats are aloof and uncaring, but as far as I'm concerned, that just means that those folks haven't met any good cats in their lives. For me, Midnight and Shadow were two of the most compassionate and caring companions a girl could ever ask for. I wondered how Shadow was really doing. He'd lost his best friend, in a manner of speaking, and though he'd shown a little reticence at first about Midnight's ghostly presence, he'd quickly adapted and had even embraced the new form of his old pal. I worried about what it would do to him once Midnight was gone again, this time permanently, but since I couldn't do anything about it, I decided to deal with that when it finally happened. I seemed to be spending a lot of time lately putting off tomorrow's worries, but it probably wasn't a bad policy to adopt.

As I locked the front door from the sidewalk, I was startled to hear a familiar voice just behind me, as though someone had been waiting for me to come out of my shop.

To my surprise, it was Sheriff Kent.

"What are you doing here?" I asked, trying not to show him just how much that he'd alarmed me.

"Do you have a second?"

"Sure thing. Is this an official police visit?" I asked.

"Yes and no," he said. "Could I buy you a drink?"

"Sheriff, are you asking me out on a date?" I asked. "I thought that you were a happily married man." It was all that I could do not to grin as I said it.

"What? No, of course not. That's not what I meant at all."

"So, I'm not good enough for you? Is that what you're saying?"

"Christy," he said, and then the sheriff paused a second before he grinned. "You're really funny. You know that, don't you?"

"I like to think so," I said.

"The drink I was going to buy you was some of Celeste's sweet tea, but we can just chat out here on the sidewalk instead, if you'd rather."

"Thanks, but I'll take the tea," I said.

We walked into the café, and the sheriff steered us to an empty corner where no one would be able to overhear us. After ordering and receiving two sweet teas, the sheriff said softly, "Your call got me thinking about what really might have happened at the Bentley farm."

"Do you think that it was homicide, too?" I asked.

"I'm not willing to commit that much yet, but I do agree that a few odd coincidences had to happen before that heater killed Silas and Summer," he said after taking a long sip of tea. "What made you think that it was more than just an accident?"

I wanted to tell him that Summer told me herself from beyond the grave, but I knew that was just going to get me locked up for a psychiatric evaluation. "I can't really say. All I know is that things just didn't add up," I said.

"You've got good instincts," he said. "I'm having a heater

expert go over that thing again carefully, and if the safety cutoff switch has been tampered with, she'll know it. I should have taken it to her in the first place, but she was busy, and I'm afraid my second choice might have missed something."

"So, you're going to treat the case as a double homicide now?" I asked.

"Whoa. Slow down, young lady. I'm not willing to say that until I've heard from my expert. Pardon me for saying so, but why do you have so much interest in this? When it was Cora and Midnight, I understood your personal involvement in the case, and I cut you some real slack, but as far as I know, you didn't have a relationship with Silas or Summer."

"That's where you're wrong. Summer came into my shop quite a bit, and we got to know each other since she came back to Noble Point." It was true, too, though perhaps not as much as I was leading him to believe. Summer had come in a few times, and if I counted her ghostly visit earlier, that made three, and that was close enough to "quite a bit" to suit me.

"Sorry, I didn't know," the sheriff said. "Still, I'd appreciate it if you'd leave the detective work to me and my staff this time."

"It can't hurt me asking some questions around town though, can it?"

"I'd rather you didn't," the sheriff said as he pushed his half-full glass of tea away from him.

"But you're not coming right out and ordering me to stop, are you?"

He seemed to think about that for a full minute before he spoke. "I can't do that, not until I determine whether or not it was murder or just a terrible accident."

"Well then, I'm probably going to keep asking a few questions around town anyway."

"You won't drop this as a favor to me?" he asked.

"Look at it another way, Sheriff. I might get someone to

tell me something that they wouldn't say directly to you. It can only help you, if you know what I mean."

At least he smiled as he said, "That's the nicest way anyone has ever told me to stuff it since I've been the sheriff around here."

"I guess that's something, then," I said as I finished my tea. I was tempted to get a refill for the road, but my pledge to cut down had to start sometime. Maybe one glass at a time instead of three or four would be a good start. "Thanks for the drink," I said as I stood up.

"You're welcome. Watch your step, Christy," he said softly.

"Is that a threat, Sheriff Kent?" I asked.

"No, you misunderstood me. I'm just saying that if it *was* murder, the killer isn't going to be too happy about you poking your nose where it doesn't belong."

"I'll be careful," I said.

"If you run into something that's over your head, don't be afraid to call me," the sheriff said.

"That's sweet of you," I said.

"I'm doing it more for me than I am for you," he said. "Marybeth is awfully fond of you, and if something happened to you, she'd be grief-stricken."

"Got it," I said as I made my way out of the café. His motives and incentive might not have matched mine, but it was still good knowing that the sheriff had my back. I knew that I could count on Lincoln if things got too tense as well, but I hoped that I wouldn't have to call either one of them for help. I was perfectly able to field an investigation of my own without assistance from a man.

That didn't mean that I'd shun their help if I got into trouble, though. After all, as long as the killer was caught, I'd be happy, and maybe Summer could Move On to the Other Side.

I just hoped that when she left, she didn't take Midnight with her.

In the meantime, it was time to start digging.

Chapter 7

"Mr. Lake, I wonder if I might speak with you a minute?" I asked Bud Lake after he answered the doorbell at his farm. He was a grizzled old man wearing a worn flannel shirt and blue jeans that had been patched more than once. His home reflected his personal appearance: a bit run-down, needing a good coat of paint and new shingles on the roof, but still solid. How had he been able to afford to bid on the Bentley farm, given the shape of his own homestead?

"Sure. Take a seat," Bud said as he stepped out the door and took one of the rockers on the broad front porch.

I joined him, hoping that I didn't get any splinters.

After we were both settled in, he asked, "Now, what exactly can I do for you?"

"I'd like to talk to you about Silas Bentley's place," I said.

Bud frowned as he stared at his nearest neighbor's land. "That didn't turn out the way that I hoped it would," Bud said. "What do you want to know about it?"

"I understand that the bidding got a little heated," I said.

"Jack Baron is a robber and a thief," Bud said angrily.

"Don't hold back on my account," I said with a smile.

Bud took a deep breath, let some of it out, and then he spoke again. "Sorry, but it still sticks in my craw that we're going to be neighbors. Not that he's going to do any farming. I've got a hunch I'll be looking at apartments and condos before he's done with it."

"Is he really going to develop land all the way out here?" I asked. Noble Point wasn't exactly a big city full of excitement and entertainment, but it was a lot more active than the farmland where we were sitting at the moment.

Bud Lake just snorted. "Who knows what his plans are? He's been buying land around these parts for as long as I can remember."

"Does he always buy farms?" I asked.

Bud shook his head. "No, as a matter of fact, this is the first time he's done it, as far as I know. Usually he buys wooded land, comes in and cuts all of the good trees out of it, and then he resells the property for a profit." Bud clearly didn't approve of the practice, but as far as I knew, it was legal enough, if not exactly eco-friendly.

"There aren't enough trees around here to count, are there?" I asked as I looked out at the open fields.

"No, and that's what's so puzzling. I'd hoped to increase my herd of dairy cattle with Silas's spread, but that's not happening now."

"Maybe he wanted it as an investment," I suggested.

"Beats me why he'd do that. All I know is that he beat me up pretty good at that auction." Bud scowled at the porch floor for a few seconds, and then he said, "Truth be told, I wouldn't put anything past Jack Baron when there was a profit to be made. Christy, consider this fair warning. If you decide to go sniffing around that man, I'd be careful if I were you. When we were all younger, I saw him nearly beat a man to death with his bare hands over a twenty-dollar loan. He hides it better now, but there's still a beast hiding under that suit, and that's a fact."

Wow, I'd had no idea. I'd have to watch my step when I spoke to Jack Baron. But I was with Bud Lake now. I looked around his place, and I was again reminded about his limits in the land auction.

Bud must have caught what I was doing, because he said, "You're wondering how I could bid at all, aren't you?"

"I know that farming is a tough way to make a living," I said as diplomatically as I could.

"It gets harder every year," he said, "but my wife is long gone and my kids are spread out all over the country, so it's just been me for quite a while. I've managed to put a little in the bank, but not enough to do myself any good. My children have been after me for years to sell this place and come live with one of them, but I just can't seem to bring myself to do it. This is more than a job for me; running this place is a way of life. I don't know what I'd do with myself if I didn't have my herd to watch out after."

We sat there rocking in silence for a few moments before he added, "I probably sound like a grizzled old fool to you, don't I?"

"Not a bit. I'm glad there are folks like you still left around here who are willing to farm."

Bud nodded. "And getting fewer by the day," he said. "It's a real shame about Silas and his daughter. No matter what happened in our past, they both deserved better than what they got in the end."

"You must miss your friend," I said.

"Of course I do. It's no secret that Silas and I had our share of friendly squabbles over the years, but I'll surely miss arguing with him."

This was news to me. "I didn't know that you two didn't get along."

"That's not what I meant. Christy, I'm not good at explaining things; I never have been. Most of it was just in good fun, kind of an entertainment for the two of us. Summer was the only reason we ever really argued, and that was a long time ago."

This was a bit of gossip that I hadn't heard yet. "What happened with her? Do you mind sharing it with me?"

"I can't see how it can do any harm telling you about it now. It's all water under the bridge now. My boy David was all set to go off to the Air Force Academy, but Summer had other plans for him. She told him that she was pregnant with his child the week before he was supposed to leave. David gave up his spot at the academy, and two weeks later, it turned out that it was all just a false alarm. You see, she didn't want him to leave her behind. The real tragedy of it all was that a month later, they broke up, and David lost out on a future that he'd dreamed about all his life."

"What's your son doing now?" I asked, caught up in the drama of the past.

"He's been dead eight years come June the twelfth," Bud

said. "Like I said, it was all another lifetime ago. I always said that living in the past was for dreamers and fools." He must have realized how that sounded, because he quickly added, "Like I said, it all happened a long time ago, and I couldn't be more surprised that I'm the only one who's still here. None of it really matters anymore now that David's gone." He took a deep breath, and then let it out slowly before he spoke again. "All in all, I'm sorry for what happened to Silas and Summer, and that's a fact. It's a hard life, and most times nobody ever gets a happy ending." Was that a tear in his eye as he mentioned his son's name again? Bud Lake stood up abruptly, and as he headed inside, he said, "Christy, it doesn't do anybody any good bringing up the past. I don't want to talk about it anymore."

"I understand," I said, but I was talking to myself. Bud was gone.

I hadn't known Summer all that well since she'd moved back into town, but the woman I knew now didn't seem capable of doing that to Bud's son. What had really happened between them?

I walked back to my car, and when I got there, I found Midnight sitting on the hood, as though he were warming himself in the fading sunlight.

Summer was standing nearby, and I could swear that she was crying.

"It's not true," Summer said through her tears. "I never would have tricked David like that. I loved him."

"How long were you eavesdropping?" I asked her.

"I heard everything," she admitted. "Something was pulling me here. I didn't want to hear all of the awful things that Bud Lake just said about me. I didn't do what he accused me of doing. I was just as torn up by what happened as David was."

"You heard Bud yourself. He never believed you," I said.

"How do you make a man see the truth when he's determined to believe in a lie? It's absolutely true that I got pregnant back then, and *David* insisted that he stay behind with me. I did everything I could to talk him out of staying, but he wouldn't listen to me. When I lost that baby, I thought that I'd died. It crippled something inside of us, driving a wedge between us that neither one of us could get past. *He* broke up with *me*, by the way, but Bud never could believe that it was anybody's fault but mine."

"It sounds as though he had a reason to wish you harm," I said.

Summer looked shocked by the statement. "He might not have liked us much, but he wouldn't *kill* us. Dad never did anything to him."

"He told me that they didn't get along, either," I said. "I can't strike Bud's name off my list, not with the motive that he just gave me."

"I guess not," Summer said reluctantly. "Christy, how long do I have to pay for mistakes I made when I was just a stupid kid who thought that she was in love with the boy next door?"

I decided not to point out that she might have already paid the biggest price that she could because of her actions. It wouldn't serve any purpose at that point.

After a moment, Summer asked, "So, who's next on your list?"

"Are you and Midnight planning to follow me around from suspect to suspect?" I wasn't all that keen on having a pair of silent, ghostly tails on me the entire time that I was investigating.

"I don't think so. I'm so tired," she said softly.

"Then go wherever it is that you go and let me handle this myself," I said.

She hesitated a moment, and then Summer asked, "But what if I can't come back?"

"Then know in your heart that I'll be doing everything in my power to find your murderer," I said. "I realize that it might not seem like much, but it's the best that I can do."

"It means more than you could possibly know," she said, and then Summer flickered away into nothingness. It surprised me a little when Midnight stayed behind.

"Is there something else on your mind?" I asked him.

He looked at me plaintively, and then he said, "Mrwerer."

"I'm doing the best that I can," I said. I knew from Midnight's tone of voice that he was getting impatient with me, but I was doing all that I could.

"Mrew," he said, and I had the feeling that he understood. Sometimes, when he'd been with me on This Side, he'd done that, accepting me for what he considered my limitations. It never failed to make me laugh, and I grinned again.

"I miss you, you old rascal," I said.

As I waited for his response, I heard the whisper of a purr coming from his spot on my car hood, and then he was gone.

It appeared that I was on my own again.

It took me half an hour to track Jack Baron down, but even after I cornered him coming out of Celeste's café, I was no further along in my investigation than I had been before.

"Mr. Baron, may I have a moment of your time?" I asked him on the sidewalk near Memories and Dreams.

"Why?" he asked.

"It's about Silas Bentley's place," I said.

Baron frowned. "What about it?" Any guise of civility was now quickly displaced by suspicion.

"Don't you usually buy forested land?"

"It's none of your business what I buy and why," he said.

I wasn't about to give up that easily, though. "I have to tell you, it's raised a few eyebrows around Noble Point."

"Who exactly are you, young lady?" he asked as he stared hard at me.

"I'm just an interested citizen," I said.

Jack Baron frowned at me as he shook his head. After a few moments, he nodded with clear satisfaction. "You run that thrift shop," he said as he pointed toward Memories and Dreams.

"I do," I said, "though I prefer to refer to it as an eclectic, gently used store."

"Whatever," he said as he waved a hand in the air. "So, what business is it of yours that I bought the Bentley place?"

"I was friends with Summer," I said, repeating the lie again. Or was it a lie? Had we begun to develop a friendship since she's Crossed to the Other Side? It was possible, I supposed, to make friends with a ghost.

"It's a shame about what happened to her, but I had nothing to do with that."

"Why were you so desperate to get that land?" I asked him yet again.

"Good evening," he said as he brushed past me, refusing to answer my questions. Jack Baron was going to be tougher to crack than Bud Lake had been, but I wasn't about to give up. If he wouldn't tell me what he was up to, I'd just have to use some other resources to figure it out. Once I had a motive for him buying the land, it might just help me uncover the reason for committing those two murders. One of the good things about running Memories and Dreams was that it gave me a wildly diverse set of contacts in town and out. Maybe one of my customers could help me track down the truth. In the meantime, I had two more suspects to talk to, and it was beginning to get late. I had a choice. Either I could try to find Stick Oakhurst in town or track Summer's cousin, Jan, down in Tryon's Gap. I decided to opt for the closer of the two suspects and went to Stick Oakhurst's place.

Only he wasn't there.

The porch was dark, so I went back to my car after no one answered the door, and I jotted down a quick note to leave for him.

Mr. Oakhurst,

I need to speak with you about Silas Bentley as soon as possible. If you get this too late tonight, I'll be at Memories and Dreams tomorrow morning. This is important.

Christy Blake

I hated being so cryptic, but I had to give him a reason to come and find me, and if that note didn't do it, I didn't know what might.

It appeared that I had time to find Jan Billings tonight after all.

Unfortunately, she wasn't home, either. This was getting frustrating, especially since I'd just driven half an hour to Tryon's Gap specifically to see her. I wrote out another note much like the one I'd left for Stick Oakhurst, and I slid it just inside her door so she wouldn't miss it. Hopefully at least one of them would respond to my summons the next day.

As I was walking back to my car, one of Jan's neighbors called out to me from across the street.

"She's not there," the older lady said helpfully. She was wearing a housecoat like my grandmother had once worn, and her hair was up in curlers. I thought for a second that I'd flashed back to the fifties.

"Do you happen to know when she'll be back?"

"How on earth would I know that?" she asked, clearly surprised by my question.

"I don't know. I was just hoping to get lucky," I replied with a friendly grin.

"Are you two friends?" the woman asked me. "I've never seen you here before."

I was willing to bet that she didn't miss much, either. "Actually, we've never met. I was friends with her cousin, Summer, though."

The woman's smile faded quickly into a frown. "That was tragic, wasn't it? She was so young when she died."

"Young enough," I said.

"You'll have to forgive me," she said. "When you get to be my age, anyone under sixty is still a pup, if you know what I mean."

"I don't know yet, but I wouldn't mind finding out someday," I said. "What can you tell me about Jan?"

She seemed to consider my question for a few seconds before she replied, "Well, I can't tell you when she'll get home tonight, but I can share *something* interesting with you about her."

"You've got my attention," I said.

"She's leaving us," the woman said.

I'd heard a great many euphemisms for death in my life, and the woman's sadness seemed to indicate that was indeed what she implying. "She's dying?"

"Heavens no. At least not as far as I know," she said. "What makes you say something like that?"

"You said she was leaving," I explained.

"Leaving town, not the planet," the woman said.

"When is she going?"

"As soon as she wraps up everything with the estate," she explained. "From what she told me this morning, it shouldn't be more than a few days until she's gone."

"Do you happen to know where she's going?" I asked.

"Not a clue. In fact, she's been quite mysterious about it whenever I ask her. We'll miss Jan around here. She's been an interesting neighbor."

"In what way?" I asked, honestly curious about the description.

"Why, in every way," the woman said.

I heard a man's voice coming from inside her house. "Esther, are you out there? Your show's about to start."

Ester's face lit up like there were fireworks. "Oh, I have to go. Sorry."

"Thanks for chatting," I said.

As she rushed inside, she waved a hand back at me. "You're most welcome."

That was interesting. Why was Jan leaving town? Was it directly tied to her new inheritance, or was there another reason she was picking up roots and taking off? I hoped to find out, but evidently, my information-gathering opportunities were over for one night. It was time to head back to the house I shared with Marybeth in Noble Point and try to relax a little before I had to start over again the next day.

Chapter 8

"Hey there," Marybeth said as I walked into the house that we shared. "I was about to call out a search party for you, Christy."

"Sorry. I know I should have called you, but I got hung up," I replied as I put my purse down on the counter of the old house. Her grandparents left the place to her in their wills, and after we roomed together in college, Marybeth moved there to live. Not long afterward, I came to visit her, and to my surprise, I'd ended up staying.

Shadow appeared out of nowhere and began to head-butt me with affection. "Hey there," I said as I slid my hand gently down his back.

"Mrerew," he said happily.

"Don't let the rascal try to fool you," Marybeth said. "I already fed him an hour ago."

Ever since Midnight had been gone, or at least changed, I'd taken special pains to make Shadow feel loved. "I could still give him a treat," I said.

Shadow perked up even more as I went to the cabinet where we kept little treats for him. As I fed him a few small bites, Marybeth said with a smile, "If you keep that up, you're going to have to put him on one of my diets with me." My best friend was constantly trying to lose those last fifteen pounds, with little or no success; each new diet she tried was odder than the last. Fortunately, at the moment, she was in between diets, so we were both eating heartily.

"Speaking of food," I said, "have you had dinner yet?" I could smell Italian spices in the air. "And more importantly, was there any left over for me?"

"There's some lasagna in the fridge," she said. "Help yourself. You were late, and I didn't feel like waiting." The last was said with a good-natured grin. We'd hold up many things for each other, but rarely when food was involved.

"Wonderful." I took the pan out and dished out a healthy portion. As the microwave oven worked its magic, I grabbed some cold milk and set a place at the table where Marybeth was working on her latest project, a collage of photos from her younger days.

"Look how handsome my grandfather was," she said as she held up a sepia photo of a dashing young man with a magnificent mustache.

"Wow, he was a real looker, wasn't he?"

"My grandmother agreed with you," she said. "She used to love to tell the story about how she first caught his eye. Did I ever tell you about it?"

"No, but I'd love to hear it," I said as the timer on the microwave dinged. "Hang on one second, okay?"

"I don't have to wait until you're seated to tell you," Marybeth said. "Every year, Noble Point used to have a pie-baking contest for charity. Men would bid on the pies and then share a slice with the bakers. Well, my grandmother was no fool, so she talked to his mother and discovered that the young man had a taste for really savory pie. He never had a sweet tooth, but my oh my, could he put away meat and potatoes. My grandmother guarded this information with her life, and the day of the auction, she was the only girl in town who presented a pie that wasn't sweet at all. In her efforts to make sure that he could pick her pie out of the dozen surrounding it, according to her, she used more onions and garlic than anyone ever should. Well, just as she planned, my grandfather chose her pie over all of the others. One taste though, and she knew that she should have practiced a little before she put her pie up for sale. She claimed that after one bite apiece, their breath was so strong that it could knock a bird out of the sky from twenty paces."

"That's terrible," I said, loving Marybeth's flair for the dramatic when she told stories.

"You'd think so, right? But that's not what happened at all. They both became kind of pariahs all that day, and no one could stand talking to either one of them for more than a few minutes at a time. They were forced to spend their time together because of that pie, and by the end of the day, my grandfather was just as smitten with my grandmother as she was with him. Hang on, I have a picture that was actually taken on the day I've been telling you about."

"You're kidding. I'd love to see it."

Marybeth started digging through boxes of photos as I ate the excellent lasagna. It was delicious, with just the right ratios of meat to sauce to noodles. "You've outdone yourself with this one, my friend."

Marybeth looked up for a second and grinned. "I started with a recipe from the Food Network and decided to play with it a little. I like mine better."

"I don't know how theirs tasted, but so do I," I said.

"Got it," she said loudly all of a sudden. It scared Shadow off his pillow, and he raced down the hall. "He's a little jumpy, isn't he?"

"He's got a right to be, doesn't he?" I asked as I went after him.

"Now I feel bad," Marybeth said.

I patted her shoulder. "You shouldn't. I've got a hunch I know right where he is."

I looked down the hallway toward the bookcases where I'd first discovered Midnight upon his return, and sure enough, Shadow was up there watching over me, all alone.

"Do you want to come down and rejoin us, or are you happier up there?"

"Mrrwr," he said, and I knew that there would be no budging him from his perch for a while.

"Suit yourself," I said.

When I got back into the kitchen, Marybeth said, "I can't believe I spooked him like that. I'm so sorry."

"I've got a hunch that he wanted some time alone anyway," I said as I sat back down at my food. There were a few bites left, and I debated getting more, but I decided that discretion might be the better part of valor this time. "So, let's see that photograph."

She held it up, and I saw the handsome man again, this time standing beside a young woman who was smiling remarkably like one of my cats. "It means a great deal more after you've heard the story, doesn't it?" I asked her.

"I hope so. After all, I come from a long line of storytellers," she said.

"Did any of them ever write one down?" I asked.

"No, we've all preferred the oral tradition of tales," she said. "I heard you made quite a scene at the auction today."

"When I relocated here, you never told me about the efficiency of small-town gossip."

She grinned at me as she said, "If I'd told you the truth, you might not have come."

"You ended up in Noble Point, Marybeth. Where else would I be?"

Her grin faded as she said, "I've actually thought about that a time or two. Maybe Midnight would still be alive if you hadn't come here to stay with me."

It was unlike her to be so morose. "Marybeth, listen to me. In many ways, Midnight is still very much with me." I'd never shared with her the fact that my ghost cat had come back to me. Marybeth didn't believe in ghosts, two legged or four legged, and I couldn't stand the thought of her doubting that my cat was really there. Even though nobody else could see him, there was no doubt in my mind that Midnight had returned. This time, he'd even brought a new friend along with him.

"Maybe so, but it's still not the same as having him here with you."

"I believe that we all have a certain amount of time in this world, and Midnight's was up. If it hadn't been a killer doing him in, it would have been something else."

"Do you really believe that?" she asked me.

"I do, with all of my heart."

"I wouldn't want to know when the sand in my hourglass was about to run out, would you?" Marybeth asked with a bit of a shiver.

"No way. I want to be surprised."

"I thought so. Now, back to the auction. I heard that there was a woman there who practically wrestled you to the ground for a box of trinkets that wasn't worth ten dollars."

I wasn't all that surprised that the story had been embellished in the telling. Marybeth wasn't the only natural storyteller in town. "Trust me, it wasn't anything quite that dramatic."

"But you got a lot of worthless stuff for your shop, right?"

I realized that I still had the money from Vera Covington in my pocket, so I took it out and fanned it in front of her. "Does that look worthless to you? As a matter of fact, I've already made a rather handsome profit on one of my finds."

"Wow! How are we going to blow it?" Marybeth asked as her face lit up. "After all, it has to be considered some kind of a windfall, doesn't it?"

"I'm plowing it back into the shop," I said as I stuffed the money back into my pocket.

"What did you find that was so valuable, anyway?" she asked.

"There was an engagement ring wrapped tightly in one of the newspapers I found," I said.

"How odd."

"You'd better believe it. That woman you heard about is named Lucy, and I have a hunch she did it herself so she could buy what looked like a worthless box and make a killing on it. She was furious when she found out that I found the ring myself. Well, Lincoln did, at any rate."

"That's right, I'd almost forgotten that you two went together. How did the big auction date go, then?" she asked with a twinkle in her eyes. Marybeth had dated Lincoln in high school, but when she'd left for college, they decided that they'd both be better off as friends, and as soon as I hit town, the man had decided that I was the right girl for him, of all things.

I was still yet to make up my mind about that, though.

"I wouldn't really call it a date," I said.

"I'll bet Lincoln would. Did you have fun?"

"As a matter of fact, beyond a few odd things happening, it was really rather nice."

"I'll bet it was," she said. "So, is that why you were so late?"

"No, we split up hours ago."

"Were you off somewhere selling the ring, then?"

"No," I said. "We did that right after we had lunch together."

"Then I repeat my original question. Why were you so late getting home? Not that it's any of my business. I'm just curious, that's all. You know me."

I had to make a decision, and I had to do it quickly. Would it be possible to explain that I was involved in another murder investigation without bringing up the fact that my ghost cat was involved again? I'd held it from Marybeth so far, but I hated keeping so many secrets from her. I decided to share part of the truth with her, just not my motivation. Hopefully it would work. "I've been looking into what happened at the Bentley farm."

"Do you mean today at the auction?" she asked as she searched through another box of photos.

"No, I'm talking about when Silas and Summer died," I said quietly.

"It was an accident," my best friend said quickly. "Everyone knows that."

"Everyone just might be wrong," I said. "Your uncle even thinks that it's a possibility."

Marybeth laughed a little uncertainly, as though she wasn't sure that I was serious or not. When I didn't respond in kind, she said, "You're a braver woman than most people around here, Christy. My uncle is not fond of folks nosing around in his business."

"I've done it before though, remember?"

"You had a stake in that one," Marybeth said. "What's the tie this time?"

And with one simple question, it all came down to how I

chose to respond. I wanted to tell her about Midnight, but in the end, I just couldn't bring myself to do it. "Summer came into Memories and Dreams a few times, and we were just starting to become friends. It makes me angry that someone might have stepped in and ended her life as we were getting to know each other."

"But doesn't that go against your philosophy that we each only have a certain number of days available to us?" she asked.

It was a fair question. I just wished that I had a good answer for her. In the end, I decided to take the easy way out. "Hey, I never said that I was consistent, did I?"

"No, but then again, what fun would that be?" she asked. "Do you need any help solving the case? I'm up for a little detecting if you are."

"I thought that you already *had* a full-time job," I said. Marybeth was a pharmaceutical drug rep, and she loved the freedom it gave her. I knew that she worked hard at her job and that she was very good at it, but her product line wasn't all that extensive, nor was her territory all that expansive. It gave her some time for herself, but she usually guarded every second of it very carefully.

"I do, but things are slow right now. I could give you a few days, if you'd like a hand."

"That's awfully sweet of you, but you don't really have a stake in this, do you?"

"No, but I'd love to help my best friend snoop around in other people's lives. Do I need a better reason to help than that?"

"Not that I can think of," I said. "Unfortunately, I've already spoken to all of the suspects that I could find today. I left a couple of notes for them to come by Memories and Dreams tomorrow, but who knows if they will."

"Tell you what," Marybeth said as she took out her mobile phone and started flipping from screen to screen on it. "Let me take a quick peek at tomorrow's schedule." It was certainly much more than just a cellphone. She even read books on it, though how she managed that I'd never know. I loved paperbacks every now and then, especially when they found their way into the store, but I was quickly being converted to reading on my e-reader. It was handy having my library with me wherever I went, and I'd been known to scan a chapter or two of a particularly engrossing book while I was waiting for customers to miraculously appear in my shop. Perhaps the time I read would have been better spent actually trying to bring new customers in, but I didn't begrudge myself the chance to read a few words of fiction every now and then.

She continued. "I can wrap things up tomorrow by lunchtime, so if no one comes looking for you, we'll go to them. What do you think about that?"

"I'd love the company, to be honest with you," I said, "though Lincoln might be a little jealous."

"Of us spending time together?" she asked. "Surely he's not that possessive already."

"No, I meant that he likes sleuthing with me. He was a great help when I was working on the last pair of murders."

"Invite him along, then," she said. "You know what they say, the more the merrier and all of that."

"I've got a hunch that he'll be busy tomorrow afternoon," I said.

Marybeth winked at me. "He doesn't want to spend time with an old girlfriend and a new one at the same time, is that what you're saying?"

"Slow down there. I never said that Lincoln and I were dating."

"You went to the auction together, didn't you?" she asked.

"Yes, but…"

"No buts. Did you eat together afterwards?" Marybeth pressed on.

"That depends. Can you really call grabbing a quick bite at Celeste's a meal?"

"You bet I can, when it suits my purposes. Christy, whether you like it or not, you and Lincoln are on your way to becoming a couple."

"A couple of what?" I asked her with a grin. I wasn't interested in getting serious at the moment, with Lincoln or anyone else.

"A couple of old fogies, given the glacial speed this relationship is moving. Step it up."

"I'll take that under advisement," I said.

She laughed loudly. "You will not. Are you going to be up long tonight?"

"It's still relatively early. Why, what did you have in mind?"

"I picked up the new Amy Adams movie today, and I thought it might be fun watching it together." She looked at my empty plate. "I don't suppose you still have room for popcorn, do you?"

"When have you ever seen me turn popcorn down? You're going to melt the butter while I pop it, right?"

"What use is it without butter?" she asked with just the right amount of disdain.

"I was just checking. I'll start the popcorn, and you grab the butter."

It wasn't going to work out though, at least not immediately.

My cellphone rang, and I thought about ignoring it, but then I saw that Lincoln was calling me. I put the container of popcorn kernels back in the freezer where we kept it as I showed the display to Marybeth. "Do you mind?"

"Just don't be long," she said. "I've been wanting to see this since it came out in theaters."

"Okay, I promise," I said as I moved out onto the front porch where I could get a little privacy. "Lincoln, it's nice to hear from you."

"I just wanted to see how your investigation was going so far," he said.

After I described my successes as well as my failures to him, he said, "That's a good start. Listen, I can't do anything in the afternoon, but I'd be glad to lend a hand tomorrow morning if you need me."

Suddenly I had more help being offered than I needed. "I appreciate the offer, but I've got things covered, at least for now."

There was a moment's pause, and then he said a little gruffly, "Of course. That's fine. I just wanted to make the offer."

"Hold on a second. Marybeth's offered me her assistance tomorrow afternoon, so I've already decided to close the shop a little early. If I left in the morning too, there wouldn't be any point of even opening up. Besides, I'm hoping that Jan and Stick make their way to Memories and Dreams without me chasing them down across three counties. I've got a hunch that it will be a lot less intimidating to them if we chat at my shop instead of on their doorsteps."

"You don't think that they're in on it together, do you?"

I hadn't honestly thought about having multiple killers until just then. "No, at least I didn't consider it until you mentioned the possibility. Why, is there something you know that I don't?" I paused a few seconds, and then I added, "Before you make a flip response to my comment, remember that you're still trying to woo me, sir."

"That changes everything," he said, and I could practically hear the smile in his voice. "No, I don't have any information that you don't, at least not regarding your investigation."

"Lincoln, you don't mind that Marybeth's going to help me some, do you?"

The attorney said lightly, "No, I get it. Just know that I'm here if you need me. I was in on this case from the start, so I'd kind of like to see it all the way through, if you know what I mean."

"I promise, the first chance I have to use your extensive detective skills, I'll call you."

"Be sure that you do. In the meantime, have a nice night, Christy."

"I hope you have one as well," I said.

When I walked back inside, Marybeth was sitting on the couch wrapped up in another book. "That was much faster than I expected."

"We're not a pair of teenagers fighting over who hangs up first," I said with a laugh as I tossed a light pillow at her. "I thought we were going to watch a movie."

"We are," she said, "but popcorn comes first."

"It wouldn't be a movie without it, would it?" I asked as I restarted the process of making it.

"Not in my opinion. What did Lincoln have to say about being replaced?"

As I added oil and popcorn to the microwavable dish, I said, "He's not being replaced, at least not on a full-time basis. There's no reason in the world that I can't use both of you, if the need arises."

"No reason at all," Marybeth said as she added real butter to a small pan she used just for the purpose of melting butter for our popcorn.

"Good, I'm glad that we got that settled."

After the popcorn was finished, I divided it into two bowls, and Marybeth poured the melted butter over them in equal portions. At least she claimed that they were equal, but since she poured the butter, I got to pick which bowl was mine. You can trust me when I say that I took few decisions in my life more seriously.

As the movie began to play and we settled into our seats, Shadow jumped up into my lap. He wouldn't touch a kernel of popcorn if he was dying of hunger, but he still had to put his nose in the bowl to see what I was eating. I nestled the bowl at my side and ate with one hand as I stroked him lightly with the other. He seemed to enjoy it for ninety seconds before he leapt off the couch and went in search of something more entertaining than two women watching a romantic comedy.

I wondered where Midnight was at that moment and if he was safe and happy. It was probably a ridiculous way to feel about a cat that had already passed away, but I couldn't keep myself from it, and I decided that it was perfectly okay for me to worry about him, too. After all, I didn't love him one ounce less since he'd become a ghost, so why *wouldn't* I worry about him?

The movie was delightful, but it failed to completely capture my attention. I had murder on my mind, and too many suspects who might have done the dirty deeds.

I finally decided to call it an early night as soon as the end credits rolled, and I went into my bedroom upstairs, hoping to find Midnight waiting for me there.

Unfortunately, not even Shadow was there to greet me when I walked in, and I settled in for what I hoped was a dreamless night.

Chapter 9

I'd just been open the next morning for ten minutes when I spotted a familiar face lingering outside of Memories and Dreams. She was clearly working up her nerve to come inside, but after watching her pace back and forth for a full minute, I decided to take matters into my own hands.

"Myra, are you coming inside, or are you just out there standing guard?"

"What would I be guarding out here?" she asked, clearly puzzled by my question.

"You wouldn't be, but then again, I don't understand why you'd be afraid to come into my shop." I had a sudden thought. "You're not waiting for someone, are you?" I looked around for Lucy, but if she was nearby, she was too good at hiding for me to spot her.

"I'm here all alone," she said in a strong, definitive manner that sounded a bit rehearsed to me.

"Got it. So, are you coming in or not?"

"Of course I am," Myra said. She took a deep breath as she started to follow me inside the building, hesitating at the front door, and I found myself wondering if she knew that Memories and Dreams was haunted. Or was it? I used to associate haunted houses with ghosts that were bound to their buildings with some supernatural tether, while Midnight, and now Summer Bentley, seemed to come and go at will, following me around the county like a pair of long lost puppies. I was glad that I hadn't said that last bit aloud. I didn't know how Summer would feel being associated with canines, but I had a pretty good hunch that Midnight would have been peeved by it. My formerly living cat was many things, both in this life and the next, but doglike was not among them.

I must have been quiet for too long, because when I looked up, I found Myra staring at me oddly. "Is there something wrong?" I asked.

"That's what I was about to ask you. You kind of went away there for a few seconds, Christy."

"Somebody must have just walked across my grave," I said, immediately regretting my choice of words. I had too much contact with the Other Side to make glib comments like that. "Is there anything in particular that you're looking for today, Myra?"

"I don't know for sure. It's hard to say. I suppose that I'm in the mood for something large," she finally said.

What an odd request. I'd had people come in asking for quite a few strange things since I'd been at Memories and Dreams, including the man who'd come by desperately looking for cows recently, but no one in my memory had ever asked for anything strictly by its size. "I have a dancing jellybean in back," I said. "It's nearly eight feet tall."

"Nothing *that* large," she said, admonishing me as though I'd forgotten the rules to a game that I'd never played before.

"You're going to have to help me out, then. Your parameters are kind of foggy."

"I should explain," she said. "My aunt Ramona is turning sixty next week, and she has everything in the world that she could ever want."

"Wow, it must be really nice being Aunt Ramona," I said.

"I suppose that it is. At any rate, for the last few years she's preferred odd gifts that are unique, the bigger the better, to some extent. One rule is that it has to fit on one of her curio shelves, so that tops it off at three feet. I must also add that the gaudier the better."

Wow, this was going to be fun. I had a host of white elephant items that were usually just useful for games of Dirty Santa where each person tried to stick the next one with the most useless gift imaginable. "Follow me," I said as I led her to the section of the shop where I kept my oddities.

"My, that's quite a selection you've got here," she said as she picked up a hand-carved-and-painted gnome over two feet tall. This particular gnome was clearly drunk, a handcrafted piece of Americana that hadn't found a proper home since it had first walked through my door.

"I see that you've made a connection with Harry," I said.

"Is that his name?" she asked with repugnance.

"Not officially, but that's what I like to call him. Would you like to take him home with you? I can make you a good deal."

"No, I'm afraid Harry will have to stay with you a little longer," Myra said after a moment's hesitation. "How about this?"

The item she was referring to was a ceramic rooster that was covered in decoupaged old red bandanas from top to bottom. "What's his name?" she asked.

"I have no idea," I said. "Why, is that important?"

She looked a little flustered as she shook her head. "No, not at all. I just assumed that since you named the gnome, this would have a name as well."

"You're in luck," I said with a grin. "You get naming rights yourself if you buy it today."

"It's perfect," she said.

I couldn't believe that *this* was what she'd settled on, but I wasn't about to talk her out of her purchase. I'd never been a fan of the rooster, and if I were being honest about it, I would have considered paying her to get it out of the shop. "Would you like a bag, or will you take it as it is?"

"Oh, that won't do," she said. "Didn't I say? My aunt doesn't live around here. I need it wrapped carefully and boxed up. You do that as well, don't you?"

"Of course, for a slight additional fee," I said. She hadn't started haggling yet, and maybe she was one of those blessed folks who took a price tag as a final statement rather than a place to start negotiations. There were more of her kind in the world than I ever would have expected before becoming involved in Memories and Dreams, and I was thankful for every last one of them I met.

"Of course," she said. "How much extra would it be?"

I quoted her a flat fee, and happily, she agreed without hesitation. "That would be perfect. I have just one more request," she said, and I wondered what it could be. I didn't have long to wait. "I noticed those nice packing boxes you picked up at the Bentley farm auction. Since I'm paying full price for the rooster, would you mind using one of those boxes for the gift?"

"I can probably do that, if I can sort them out," I said, wondering why she was making such an odd request.

"It's important to me, so if you can't find one in particular, I'm afraid that there's not going to be a sale after all."

"Which one did you want?" I asked, trying not to show that I was growing more and more suspicious by the second. I was beginning to doubt the existence of her aunt, and instead, I was wondering if this was all a ruse just to get the box. If it was, Lucy couldn't be far away from the scheme.

"While I was at the Bentley place, I noticed that one of the boxes had a small red X marked on the back of it," she said. "That's the one that I want."

"If I can find it, it's all yours," I said. "This might take a few minutes. Would you like to come back in ten minutes and pick it up after you pay for it?"

"No, I'm happy to wait right here for it," she said.

"Okay. Let's take care of the paperwork, and then I'll wrap it for you."

"Excellent," she said, clearly relieved that I didn't seem suspicious. I wanted to get this woman into a poker game. She would be terrible at bluffing.

After I collected her money, happy for the infusion of cash into the business, I handed her a receipt and told her, "I'll be as quick as I can. Feel free to look around some more in the meantime. Maybe you'll even find something that you're interested in for yourself."

"Perhaps," she said, and I moved in back to hunt that box down.

One thing was certain; there was no way that Myra was getting the box in question before I had a chance to look at it myself.

I thought I'd found it in my pile of boxes, but when I searched the exterior of the box, there were no red Xs present, at least not any that I could find. After digging a little deeper though, I found the one that I was looking for. The only difference between it and its twin was the small red X, so I knew that I had a winner. I picked it up and studied it as closely as I could, but for the life of me, I couldn't find anything that made it extraordinary. Why would Myra, or most likely Lucy, want a box from the auction and not its contents? I'd been under the impression that Lucy had been after the engagement ring hidden in the wrapping paper, but this made me wonder if she'd even known about it.

I probably *should* have packed that rooster in the box she wanted. Myra was certainly paying me for the privilege. But I just couldn't bring myself to do it. I put the box in question beside its near twin, and then I grabbed a red marker I kept for special sale prices. Matching the X as closely as I could in size, location, and structure, I was quite satisfied with my forged results. I blew on it for a moment to dry the ink, and then I carefully packed the rooster into the fake box before I forgot which was which. Okay, the box wasn't fake; it was as real as the other one, but the mark on its back was certainly not the genuine article. Instead of using wrapping I'd gotten from the Bentley auction, I grabbed some butcher paper I had on hand and made sure that the rooster could stand any transit, though by now I was certain that the only place this particular white elephant was going was straight into Lucy's hands. I felt a little bad about the deception as I taped the top securely, but if Lucy had anything to do with the murder, I'd get over that in a heartbeat. And if she hadn't? Well, she was still getting a box that I'd acquired at the auction.

Just not the one that she'd been interested in.

I compared the markings one last time after I finished my wrap job, and they were so close that I wouldn't have been able to tell them apart myself if I hadn't shoved the rooster into the wrong box before the marker ink could thoroughly dry.

Putting on my happiest expression as I walked out of the back with the wrapped barnyard animal in hand, I gave it to Myra. "Here you go, guaranteed to make just about any journey in one piece. Did you find anything else while you were waiting?"

"No, but I must say, you've got quite an eclectic collection here for sale, don't you?"

"That's what we specialize in," I said. "Tell your neighbors and friends."

Myra clearly didn't get me, but she offered a slight smile, anyway. "Of course," she said.

Once she was gone, I wasn't sure how long I had before she discovered that she had the wrong box, but I was betting that I'd hear from her or Lucy before too long.

It was time to search the box and see if there was anything that I missed the first time I'd examined it.

I studied that box again carefully, both inside and out, but I still didn't find anything at all remarkable about it, except for the thickness of the cardboard at the bottom. There was nothing else to do but take a razor knife to it to see if there was something that I was missing. Extending the blade, I slid it through the tape and opened all of the edges of the box up to the light of day.

I don't know what I'd been expecting to find when I opened it, but I dropped the knife when I saw what was tucked under one of the taped flaps of the box's bottom.

Chapter 10

An envelope, sealed and a little dirty, fell to the floor as I slit the tape. Could it be anything *but* what I assumed that it held? The envelope was thick, as though some great missive was tucked inside, but I had a good hunch that it wasn't holding a letter. My hands shook a little as I cut the envelope open to see if I was right.

When I looked inside, my suspicions were confirmed.

There were twenty-five well-used hundred-dollar bills there. Why would anyone hide two thousand five hundred dollars in the taped bottom of a moving box? I could have just as easily thrown the box away or given it to Myra without digging further. This must have been Ginny's hiding place for her savings, and who better to know where she stashed her money than her former best friend? It suddenly all made sense. Lucy had wanted to buy that box at auction not because of any sentimental reason, but because of what her dead friend had kept hidden inside. As I fanned the bills, I wondered who it belonged to now that Silas and Summer were gone. Was it Jan's, the sole remaining heir? No, I'd bought that box at auction fair and square, so whatever was inside it legally and rightfully belonged to me. I had no compunctions about keeping it, especially since I'd come so close to just handing it over to Myra and Lucy. I ditched the envelope and put the cash in my safe, an old unit Cora bought that still worked just fine. After that, I cut out the portion with the red X and shredded it before I disposed of the rest of the box in the trash. Let Lucy prove that I kept her from stealing it from me in the first place.

I have to give them both credit. Lucy must have been waiting somewhere close by, because Myra was back not two minutes after I'd finished covering up my discovery.

She had something with her, too.

"This isn't the right box," she said as she placed it on the counter.

"I don't know what you're talking about," I said, doing my best to keep a straight face. "It has the X you asked for and everything."

"There must be more than one box with an X on it."

"Myra, what possible difference could that make? I did as you asked. I used a box from the Bentley estate sale that had a red X on it. What more can I do?"

"You can show me the other boxes," she demanded.

"I could, but I'm not going to," I said.

"Why not? What do you have to hide, Christy?"

She was right. At this point there was no reason not to show her the remaining boxes I'd gotten at Silas's place. "Fine. Come on back with me." My anger was only a little feigned. After all, she and her friend had just tried to steal something that was rightfully mine, hadn't they?

I led her to the back, happy that I'd been so quick to destroy the evidence of what I'd found. "Help yourself. That's where I keep all of the boxes that I bring in."

I was expecting a cursory glance, but to my surprise, she sorted through the boxes with a vengeance, no doubt hoping to find the duplicate X box.

Of course she didn't find it. As she started to go through my trash where she'd find the remnants of the real box, I stepped in. "That's about enough of that. I did as you asked. What exactly were you hoping to find? Was it gone when you looked?"

"Never mind," she said, and she seemed to be satisfied at last that the moneybox wasn't there.

As she started to walk out, I said, "Hang on one second. Where do you think you're going?"

Myra looked surprised by my question. "I'm leaving, of course."

"Not until you clean up your mess," I said as I pointed to the scattered boxes all over the floor. "Don't you think that it's the least you can do to make things as good as they were when you got here?"

"Yes, that's fine," she said as she started throwing boxes into the corner. They weren't nearly as neatly stacked as they had been, but I decided not to push her any more than I had. I wanted Lucy and Myra to think that Ginny had changed hiding places, or perhaps that Silas had discovered the stash himself somewhere along the line. The last thing I wanted was for those ladies to learn that I'd just found the hidden treasure myself.

"That's good enough," I said. "I hope your aunt still enjoys her rooster."

"I'm sure that she will," Myra said as she started to walk out.

"Don't forget him," I said as I grabbed the box and put it into her hands.

"Of course," she said.

I watched as she left the shop, and just before she vanished around the corner, Lucy evidently couldn't wait to ask her about the box, because she stepped out from between two buildings while they were both still in my sight. Myra delivered the news, and after a brief snit, Lucy shrugged and the two of them walked away. Evidently they both came to the same conclusion that I'd wanted. That money, for all intents and purposes, was long gone, at least for them. They'd done everything in their power to get it, but I'd trumped them without them even being aware of it. The money itself would be nice, but thwarting their plan to steal it from me was even sweeter. At least I had a small victory that I could claim, and not only that, it allowed me to strike two suspects from my list. It was pretty clear that Myra and Lucy had been after the money, but it wasn't enough of a motive to kill Summer and Silas to get it. They were opportunists, there was no doubt about that, but that didn't make them murderers.

I still had a healthy list of potential killers, though. Cousin Jan had to be on it, and Stick Oakhurst as well. Jack Baron and Bud Lake were included, too, given their desire to buy the land Silas and his family had farmed for generations. That left me with four suspects, which wasn't a perfect number, but it was still a whole lot better than six had been.

"What's this all about?" Jan Billings asked me a little after eleven as she came into Memories and Dreams waving my note around in the air. She was painfully thin, at least in my eyes, and I wondered when she'd eaten her last carb. "What's suddenly so important about Silas Bentley?"

"Thanks for coming," I said. "I'm sorry that I missed you last night."

Jan frowned at me before she spoke again. "I'm a busy woman. Dealing with the estate has been more time consuming than you could imagine."

"Plus, I heard that you're leaving the area as soon as it's all settled."

Jan clearly wasn't pleased that I'd garnered that particular bit of information. "How could you possibly know that?"

"Word gets around," I said, not wanting to tell her that one of her neighbors had shared it with me.

"Do you want to know something? I don't really care. What's this about Silas?"

"Are you aware that his death and Summer's might *not* have been accidents?" I watched her carefully for some kind of reaction as I said it.

She gave me one, in spades. "What are you talking about? The police said that it was all just a tragic accident. If they've changed their minds, they haven't said anything to me about it."

"Their official position hasn't changed. At least not yet," I said, "but I know for a fact that some folks are suspicious about the way Silas and Summer died."

"Then they have overactive imaginations," she said. "Unless someone has any facts to back up what they're saying, I'd appreciate it if they'd all just drop it."

"Don't you want to know what *really* happened to them?" I asked.

Jan shook her head sadly. "I already know. Like I said, it was an accident."

"But what if it wasn't?"

"Christy, you don't know me very well, but I'm not a woman who deals with a lot of 'what ifs' in my life. I believe in facts, not rumors."

"Even if some of them center around you?" I asked her.

Jan looked as though she wanted to say something, but for a second I thought she was going to keep quiet. Finally though, she said, "I don't know why I'm surprised that someone's out there taking jabs at me. I was never all that close with Silas or Summer, but I didn't want to see either one of them dead. If someone did this deliberately, I hope the police catch them, but it's not my job; it's theirs."

"I just thought that you might like to know what was going on," I said. Working on sudden inspiration, I added, "I could use your help, as a matter of fact."

"Me?" she asked, looking surprised by my request. "What could I possibly do to help you?"

"Jan, you've been privy to all of Silas's papers. Have you stumbled across anything that might make you suspect anyone of foul play?"

Jan frowned. "This is getting a little too weird for my taste. How could you possibly have known about that?"

"I don't know what you're talking about. Did you find something?"

Jan nodded as she dug into her purse. "I've been carrying this around with me ever since I found it this morning. I thought about showing it the police, but I had no idea what it might mean."

"May I see it?" I asked as she pulled a grocery store receipt from her bag.

"I don't see what it could hurt," she said.

Jan handed the receipt over to me, and I noticed right away that it was dated the day of the two deaths. On the back, someone had scribbled out in capital letters "GIVE ME WHAT I WANT."

I looked up and found Jan watching me. "What does it mean, Christy?"

"I have no idea," I said, and then, as I handed it back to her, I added a little reluctantly, "You need to show this to Sheriff Kent. It might be important."

"Then again, it could be something else entirely not related to what happened to Silas and Summer in any way."

"Jan, if you're reluctant to show it to him, let me do it. I don't mind being involved."

"No, they were my family. I'll do it myself."

She started to leave when I put a hand on her shoulder. "Aren't you going to do it right now?"

"No, but I'll take care of it before I leave town for good," she said. "I promise."

I wouldn't let go of her. "I'm sorry, but that's not good enough. You need to call the sheriff right now while you're standing here with me in my shop."

She jerked her shoulder out from my grip. "Christy, I haven't taken an order from anyone since I was in grade school, and I'm not about to start now."

"Suit yourself," I said as I got out my cellphone and started to dial.

"Who exactly are you calling?" she asked me.

"Sheriff Kent," I said.

"I forbid you from doing that," she snapped, clearly agitated with me.

"Would you like to know something? I'm not so good at taking orders myself," I said with the hint of a smile. "If you push me, I *always* push back," I said.

"Kent," the sheriff said as Jan looked on, her mouth still a little open.

"If you're close to my shop, you need to get over here right now. I might have an important clue for you."

"I'm on my way," he said.

"What's going on?" Jan asked.

"He's coming over here right now."

Jan looked at her watch. "I'm sorry, but I don't have time

for this right now."

"I think you'd better make time," I said as the front door opened.

It was reassuring seeing the sheriff come in. "What have you got, Christy?"

"It's not me. Ask her," I said as I pointed at Jan.

"Here, take it," she said as she shoved the receipt at him. "I found this in Silas's papers."

He studied the receipt, and then the sheriff flipped it over. He frowned as he read the printed note, and then he looked hard at Jan. "When *exactly* did you find this?"

"Early this morning," she said. "I'm sure that it's nothing. After all, you told me yourself that what happened to them was an accident. How is this relevant?"

"I'm not sure, but I'm glad that you called it to my attention."

She looked at me smugly before she answered, "I'm happy to be of service. If that's all, I'll be going now."

"That's fine. I'm finished with you," the sheriff said.

Jan didn't wait for a response from me. She hurried out of Memories and Dreams as though the place were on fire.

"She's not a big fan of yours, is she?" Sheriff Kent asked me after Jan was gone.

"I was afraid that she wasn't going to show it to you at all, so I decided to help out a little."

The sheriff actually smiled at that. "Thanks."

"What do you think it means?" I asked. "I know that you spotted the fact that the date on the receipt is significant."

"I saw it," he agreed. "I'm just not sure where it leaves us."

"Will you at least have it dusted for prints?" I asked.

He shrugged. "I'll give that suggestion every consideration that it deserves. Now, if you'll excuse me, I've got other things on my desk at the moment that I need to take care of immediately."

"Admit it. You believe that it might have been a double homicide too, don't you?" I asked him before he could get out the door.

"What makes you think that?" he asked me.

"You came here when I called you, didn't you?"

He nodded. "It's what I do. If there's nothing else, I really do need to go."

"I don't have anything else at the moment," I said.

"I don't like where this is heading," he said. "You're really digging into this, aren't you?"

"What can I say? I really don't have much choice in the matter."

"If that were only true," he said, and then Sheriff Kent was gone.

I had mixed emotions about my talk with Jan. On one hand, she'd been pretty defensive about the mere *suggestion* that what had happened to Silas and Summer might have been anything but an accident. Then again, she'd brought that note out for me to see when she could have just as easily thrown it away and no one would be the wiser. But did that necessarily mean that she was innocent? After all, if she *had* been responsible for what had happened and she thought that I might be onto her, what better thing to do than to try to cast my suspicions on someone else? I was more confused than ever, but at least I'd managed to add something to the scant collection of evidence. I'd love to know who had written that note and what they'd meant by it, but for now, I was just going to have to live with my frustration.

As I locked the front door so I could sneak away for some lunch, I heard a voice call out to me. "Christy, hang on a second."

I turned to see Stick Oakhurst lumbering my way. He was a big man in many ways, including his booming voice.

I stepped away from Memories and Dreams and waited for him to make it over to me. He was a little out of breath, even though he hadn't come that far, or fast, either.

"One second," he said as he held up one hand after finally

making it to me. "Got to get in shape one of these days," he said, panting a little as he said it. "Got your note," he added before he had to pause again to let his breathing catch up with him.

"Sorry for being so dramatic, but it truly is important."

Stick tried to smile as he continued to breathe in and out heavily. "Can't imagine what it could be. You hungry?" he asked as he glanced over at Celeste's diner.

"As a matter of fact, I was just going to lunch," I said.

"Then let's eat together. My treat."

I wasn't sure that I wanted to be in his debt, even for the price of a meal, but it would give me plenty of opportunity to talk to him about what Summer had told me earlier. I still wasn't sure how I was going to bring it up, since I couldn't exactly tell him the real source of my information. Or could I? I had a sudden thought, and decided that it could work, if I did a good job selling it. "That would be great."

As we entered the café, Celeste started to say something to me until she noticed that I was with Stick. "Sit wherever you'd like," she finally said without much emotion in her voice.

If Stick noticed her hesitation, he didn't show it. "I've been here enough to know that, Celeste."

We found a table, and the owner approached us immediately. "Hello, Christy."

"Hi," I said. "What's good today?" I hoped that she didn't bring up my odd lunch companion, at least not until later.

"Everything," she said loudly, and I wondered why Celeste was broadcasting the information across the room.

I didn't even have to glance at the menu. "I'll have the meatloaf platter."

Celeste frowned as she replied with a softer voice, "I wouldn't do that if I were you. I had some of the meatloaf earlier, and as much as I hate to say it, Justine's a little off her game today. I'd probably have a burger instead."

I nodded in appreciation. Justine could be brilliant at the grill, but sometimes her experiments in the culinary arts were a bit outlandish for my taste. "A burger sounds great. Add some fries and sweet tea to that, would you?"

"Make that two," Stick said with a grin. "And I mean two of each for me. You can bring Christy whatever she wants. What kind of pie do you have today?"

"Chocolate cream, strawberry, and lemon custard," she said.

"Save a piece of each for me, will you? I'm not sure how hungry I'll be after I finish the first course."

"Consider it done," she said. The look Celeste gave me as she started to walk away told me that we had a lot to talk about, but I was thankful that she appeared to be willing to wait until after Stick was gone.

After we got our drinks, Stick said casually, "While we're waiting for the main event, what's so important all of a sudden? You didn't get in any more Civil War soldiers, did you?"

That was how I knew Stick in the first place. He collected vintage war toys, and his particular specialty were the small lead soldiers from the Civil War. "No, but I'll call you the second I get any in."

"Good. If it's not that then, what is it?"

"Summer Bentley and I were friends. Did you know that?" I was stretching the truth a little again, but I had to if my fabricated cover story was going to work. I had a hunch that Summer wouldn't mind. After all, I was doing this in order to find out who had murdered her and her father.

"No, I didn't realize that. Funny, I never saw you out at the farm."

It was true enough, since I hadn't been there in quite a long time before the auction. "She used to come by Memories and Dreams," I said.

"Then I'm sorry for your loss," he said almost automatically.

"Thanks. Summer told me something that was a little distressing just before she died," I said as I purposely avoided making eye contact with him. I wanted him to believe that this questioning was awkward for me, so I really had to stress how uncomfortable I was in bringing it up.

"What was it about?" Stick asked as his voice lowered a bit. I glanced up at him and saw that he was suddenly very intent on what I had to say next.

"Stick, she told me about that night at the house when you had a fight with Silas." I glanced again and caught a surprised expression shoot across his face before he quickly buried it.

"What exactly did she tell you, Christy?"

"You and Silas were arguing about him sharing something with you. What did you want half of, Stick? Summer said that you were pretty demanding about it."

Stick shook his head. "I *knew* that she heard more than she admitted," he finally said.

"It doesn't look good for you. I don't have to tell you that, do I?"

He looked startled by my statement. "Why would you say that?"

"Think about it. You were arguing with a man who was soon after murdered. That's not exactly a ringing endorsement, is it?"

"Murdered?" he asked incredulously. "Who said that Silas was murdered?"

"The police are looking into it right now," I said. I had to pretend to know more than I really did if my plan was going to work.

Stick's face went ashen. "I haven't heard about that until now."

"Why were you bullying him to share with you?" I asked, pressing the big man harder now.

Stick stood abruptly, threw a twenty on the table, and then he said loudly, "I have to go."

"What about your lunch?"

"I'll eat later," he said, and then, as he rushed out of the café, Celeste showed up with our plates.

"What's wrong with him?" she asked as she slid my plate

in front of me.

"He had to leave all of a sudden," I said.

"If I hadn't seen it with my own eyes, I never would have believed it. Christy, what did you say to that man? As far as I know, he hasn't missed a meal in his life."

And then I knew that I had to come up with something good, or I'd be forced to actually tell Celeste the truth.

Chapter 11

I chose to lie.

After all, talking about a ghostly murder victim and a returning spectral cat wouldn't make anyone feel better about my credibility.

"It wasn't anything all that dramatic," I said, trying to downplay my involvement in investigating Summer's and Silas's murders.

"We both know better than that," she said. "Do you think there's a chance that Stick will still want this?"

"I doubt it." I pointed to the twenty as I said, "At least you got paid for it."

"More's the miracle still," she said. "What am I supposed to do with all of this food?"

"You could always join me," I said.

My friend looked around her café, and she must have seen that her patrons were all happily eating and otherwise occupied at the moment. Celeste grinned at me as she said, "You know what? I think I'll do just that."

After she took the first bite of one of the burgers, she said, "Justine might take a few risks in the kitchen every now and then, but she can make a burger like nobody's business. What's with your lunch date, anyway?"

"I already told you. He just took off all of a sudden for no reason that I could see."

"We both know better than that," Celeste said as she pointed a French fry at me. "Why were you two eating together in the first place?"

"I don't suppose I could get you to accept that it was just all one big coincidence, could I?"

"Not in a million years. Come on. Spill."

"As a matter of fact, it was about something that Summer Bentley told me just before she died," I said, and then I quickly took another bite of my hamburger.

That certainly got Celeste's attention. She put the burger down on the plate, and then she looked steadily at me before she spoke again. "Christy, what are you up to?"

"Why do I have to be up to something?" I asked, and then I shoved a pair of French fries into my mouth before I said anything else.

"We haven't known each other a long time," she said, "but I still know you better than that."

I took a deep breath, and then finally, I said, "Celeste, I have a hunch that Silas and Summer didn't die by accident."

"Are you saying that it was *murder*?" she asked me in a soft voice.

"I think so, and the sheriff's quietly digging around a little, too."

"So you decided to solve the case on your own, just like you did the last time." Celeste was obviously referring to my investigation into Cora's and Midnight's murders. "Don't bother denying it. Suddenly everything all makes sense. I suppose that you've wrangled Lincoln into your investigation again too, haven't you? That's why you took him to the Bentley auction in the first place."

"Actually, at the time, it was more of a social engagement than anything else," I said, and then I suddenly felt my face blush a little. Why did admitting that seem to bother me?

"But it didn't end up that way, right?"

"Lincoln just happened to be there at the time," I said. I wouldn't hesitate to ask him for help if I needed it, but I hated dragging anyone else into my investigations. Marybeth had offered her services as well, and I had to wonder if half the world secretly wanted to be an amateur sleuth.

"Sure he did," Celeste said. "I get all of that, but what's your stake in this case?"

I decided that I'd found a good cover story, so why not stick to it? It wasn't as though Summer could deny that we were friends to anyone but me. "Summer and I were just beginning to become friends."

"I can see that," Celeste said.

"Really?" I asked.

"Sure. You both have that inquisitive nature that's bound to get you into trouble. So, what can I do to help? Did Stick do it? Is that why he rushed out of here? You didn't just accuse him of murder in my café, did you?"

"Slow down. I don't know who did it yet, and I'm certainly not ready to accuse anyone of anything," I said, trying to calm her down a little.

"But he's a suspect in your mind, right?" Celeste asked eagerly.

"Among others," I admitted.

"Why do you think that *he* might have done it?" she asked me. It was clear that Celeste wasn't above an idle speculation or two of her own.

"I don't feel comfortable going into too many details until I have more information," I said, and then I took another bite of my burger.

Celeste wasn't the least bit deterred by my comment. "At least tell me who else is on your list."

I started to say no as a knee-jerk reaction, but then I decided that Celeste just might be a font of information about the other folks on my list. She'd lived in town forever, and besides, at one time or another, I was sure that practically everyone within a hundred-mile radius had eaten a meal at her café. What could it hurt to just share the other names with her? She would be discreet if I asked her to keep our conversation quiet.

"You won't breathe a word of this if I tell you, right?" I asked.

She crossed her heart with her right index finger and thumb. "You have my word."

"Okay," I said softly. "I won't tell you exactly *why* these folks are on my list, but I'm looking at Stick, Jan Billings, Jack Baron, and Bud Lake."

Celeste whistled softly. "Wow, that's quite the roster you've got there."

"It was even longer earlier," I said, "but I've struck two

names off of it already."

"Tell me," she said eagerly.

I didn't see any reason to drag Lucy and Myra through the mud, since I was now fairly certain that neither of them had done it. "There's no reason to since I've cleared them both, at least for now. Let's focus on the names I have that are still active suspects. What do you know about them?"

She was about to speak when Sam Weatherall approached the cash register and looked around. Celeste held up one finger as she told me, "Hang on. I'll be right back."

"Remember, this is confidential," I said as she stood up.

Celeste crossed her heart again as she grinned. "I promised, remember?"

It was the best that I could ask for. If I was going to trust other people in the course of my investigation, I had to take them at their word. Otherwise, I'd just have to slog through my detective work by myself, with no help from any outsiders. That would be a lonely way to conduct a search for the real killer. As a matter of fact, it would be a poor way to live in general. In all of the times that I'd trusted people in the past, I had only been disappointed in the results on a few occasions, but I couldn't let that keep me from ever trusting anyone else again.

Frankly, I'd rather have a little heartache in my life than bitter loneliness.

Celeste came back soon enough. "Sorry about that," she said as she cleared our dishes away. I'd finished my burger and most of my fries, but she'd barely made headway into one of her hamburgers. "I'll just clean this up, and then I'll be right back."

Celeste emptied the plates into the trash, and then I watched as she put them into a plastic tub. As she did, Justine came out of the back waving her metal spatula in the air. "What was wrong with those burgers, anyway?"

"Nothing," Celeste said quickly. "They were wonderful."

Justine snorted as she peered down into the trashcan. "If they were so good, why did you just have to throw out so much food?" She looked around the dining room, and her gaze stopped on me. "Christy Blake, you *love* my hamburgers. What was wrong with this one?"

"I ate just about every bite of it," I protested.

Justine frowned as she turned to Celeste. "Is that true?"

"It is," she admitted.

"Well, I know that Stick Oakhurst didn't throw out a single bite, so what happened?"

"He had an emergency, so he had to leave before he could eat," I said quickly, trying to save Celeste from her cook's wrath.

"It must have been pretty important," she said. "Why didn't you order the meatloaf? Christy, you love my meatloaf."

Now *I* was on the spot. I didn't want to place the blame on Celeste, but I wasn't all that keen on lying to Justine, either. I could see that Celeste was about to confess though, so I decided to throw myself on the grenade. "I just wasn't in the mood for meatloaf today," I said loudly before Celeste felt as though she had to respond.

Justine surprised us both when she said, "It's just as well. To be honest with you, you made a good choice. I put way too much cumin and garlic in this batch. I thought the combination would enhance the flavor, but it overpowered it instead." She frowned for a second before she asked, "How could you possibly know that, though?" Justine sniffed the air once, and then she said, "You can smell it in the air, can't you?"

As a matter of fact, I couldn't. Instead of lying outright, though, I said, "Sorry," and left it at that.

"There's nothing for you to be sorry about," Justine said. In a louder voice, she announced, "Meatloaf is off the menu today."

Caleb Lance, an older gentleman who loved a good joke, said, "That's too bad. From the way that you just described it, it sounded perfect."

"Then you can have it all to yourself, with my

compliments," Justine said. "I'll wrap it up for you." As she turned to go back to the kitchen, she added, "Now don't you go *anywhere*. I'll be right back. And I want you back here in an hour, and I'd better smell that garlic on your breath."

"You will," Caleb said morosely.

Justine was back in a flash with a rather substantial-sized doggy bag. "There you go. I'll see you soon, Caleb."

"Bye," he said as he slid a five under his plate and carried off the spoils of his humor.

After he was gone, Justine's laugh rocked the place, and we all shared our own relieved smiles. "That man has got to learn not to joke with the people who prepare and serve his food. He reminds me of my uncle Benny. Benny would go to the most outlandish lengths to make a point. One time he wore flippers and goggles into town after a particularly heavy rain."

"That doesn't sound so bad," Celeste said, playing along.

"He'd have probably gotten away with it if it hadn't been for the reins he had in his hands."

"What did he say they were for?" Celeste asked.

"Well, Benny claimed they were for the sea horse he had parked outside of town. He claimed to ride it in after the water crested over his roof."

"And nobody believed him?" I asked.

"That was the heart of his problem; nobody *ever* believed him. When he actually won a million dollars in the lottery and moved away, it took the mailman a year before he trusted it and actually started forwarding his mail to his new address. The joke ended up being on Benny then, too, though. His winning check came in the mail, and he didn't get it until a year later."

Justine, satisfied with telling the story, returned to her kitchen, and Celeste rejoined me.

As she sat down, I said, "Justine is one of a kind, isn't she?"

"She has her quirks, but she can surely work a grill like no one that I've ever had. Now, about those names you mentioned earlier. I have some thoughts, if you're interested."

"You bet that I am," I said.

"Okay, here goes. Jan Billings is the only heir, and while I don't know the woman very well personally, I understand why she's on the list. Stick is a bit of a stretch, though."

"You don't see him as a killer?"

"It's not that. I'm sure that if he thought he had a good enough motive, he could do it. I just don't see him moving a hay bale. The man was born lazy, and there's no doubt in my mind that he'll die that way as well."

"Then you'd mark him off the list, if you could?"

Celeste thought about that for a few moments. "I wouldn't go *that* far. If there was enough money, or any reward, in it for him, I wouldn't put it past him, as sad as that is to say about someone that I know."

"What about the other two men?" I asked, hoping to get the information out of Celeste before duty called again.

"Yes, I can see Jack and Bud both doing it. I've never been a fan of either man, but their motives would be a lot different if it turned out that one of them did it."

"How so?" I asked.

"It's been said around town that Jack would kill his own grandmother if there was profit to be made from it, but for Bud, it would have to be personal. That man can hold a grudge like nobody I've ever known. It's pretty clear that after what happened between Bud's son and Summer, he could have felt justified doing *anything*."

"So then, all four people have to stay on my list of suspects," I said.

"They should. Christy, it suddenly occurs to me that I'm not very good at this. As I considered each name that you gave me, I found myself convinced that they were guilty, each in their own turn. How do you do it? It must be awful, thinking up reasons people might do bad things to each other."

"I try to focus on the justice of it," I said. "I'm not looking for revenge. I just don't want to see *anyone* getting away with murder."

"Yes, I can understand that. Well, all that I can say is good luck. If I run across anything that I think might help, I'll be sure to let you know."

"I'd appreciate it."

After I paid my bill, I walked back over to Memories and Dreams, wondering where my investigation would take me next.

I didn't have all that long to find out, though.

Jack Baron was standing there waiting for me to open as I walked back toward the shop.

Chapter 12

"What can I do for you, Mr. Baron?" I asked as I stepped around him and unlocked the front door of Memories and Dreams. I made no move to go inside, though. If I was going to speak with the gruff man, I was going to do it in public. I remembered Bud Lake's warning about the savage lurking just beneath the surface, and I promised myself that I'd be extra careful around the man.

"Please, call me Jack," he said, doing his best to sound jovial. This was a different man than the one I'd spoken with before who had been curt with me from the first moment that he opened his mouth.

"Forgive me for saying so, but you weren't quite so friendly the last time we spoke."

"That's one of the reasons that I'm here." He looked around, and then Baron added, "Could we possibly step inside and chat?"

I considered it, and then I realized that there was no justification for keeping him out on the sidewalk. "Sure thing," I said.

He walked in after me, and I switched the sign announcing that I was again open for business. I wouldn't have minded a horde of shoppers at that point, but alas, we were alone.

"You were saying?" I asked as I stepped behind the counter to put some kind of barrier between us. I didn't automatically assume that he was a murderer, but he was on my short list of suspects, so it might pay to give myself a little space in case things turned ugly.

"Christy, I came to apologize for my behavior earlier. My ex-wife wasn't right about many things while we were married, but I'm afraid that she was spot on when she used to say that it took a great deal of work to get past my attitude at first."

Evidently she'd found it too much work to continue, since

she was now his ex. "I appreciate that," I said.

"What can I say? You caught me on a bad day during a particularly tough moment."

"What happened?" I asked.

He shook his head. "It's not important. All that really matters is that I came here to say that I'm sorry. You asked me why I was so interested in the Bentley farm, and I blew you off."

"It's a fair question though, isn't it? From what I hear, you normally just buy wooded lots."

He nodded. "That's been true up to a point, but I'm getting tired of having a reputation as a tree killer, if you want to know the truth. I like to think that the land I buy and the wood I cut is good for the local economy."

"And your bank account as well," I said gently.

"Sure, I like to make a profit as much as the next man," he said as an edge of anger started to creep into his voice. "That's what business is all about. People forget that someone cut the trees on the land where their homes now stand. I don't see too many of the complainers living in tents under the stars."

"Isn't clearing enough land to build a home different somehow from buying a forest and cutting it to the ground?"

He started to frown again, but Baron suddenly caught himself and forced a determined smile to his lips. "It's a matter of semantics at that point. Trees are being lost. Anyway, that's beside the point. You wanted to know why I bought the Bentley farm. The truth is, I've been thinking about retiring, so it looked like it might be a good place for me to spend my old age."

A thousand alarms began going off in my head. I didn't believe this man for one second. "Have you ever *lived* on a farm? From what I've seen, it's more work in a month than most folks can do in a lifetime."

"I'm getting rid of the livestock and the crops," he said dismissively. "You're right. That's a great deal more work than I want to do."

"Then why buy a farm in the first place?"

"Maybe I just like the view, but it's not all that important. As I said, I have my reasons." He rubbed his hands together as he added, "Well, I've delivered my apology, but like I said, that's only one of the reasons I came by. I understand that you're poking around into what happened at the farm. Is that right?"

"I'm just curious. If you don't mind me asking, where exactly did you hear that?"

"Does it matter? Let's just say that a little bird told me. To be honest with you, I agree. There's something fishy about what happened to Silas and Summer."

Was it possible that this man was my ally? I couldn't believe that. He had to have his own agenda. "What makes you say that?"

"I knew Silas pretty well. I'd been trying to buy his place for years, but he kept turning me down. We weren't exactly buddies, but I had a grudging respect for the man. We drank more than our fair share of homegrown booze together over the years, and I can tell you for a fact that he was not stupid, not by any means. There is no way that he'd be careless enough to stack hay by that heater's vent."

"Do you have any ideas about who might have done it?" I asked, still catching my breath from this startling turn of events.

"If you ask me, it has to be either Bud Lake or Stick Oakhurst," he said. "I'd start with Bud, but if that doesn't work out, then I'd try taking a look at Stick."

"Are you accusing your rival for the property of murder?"

"All I'm saying is that he was desperate to get his hands on that land. He even threatened me before the auction. Did you know that?"

"This is the first I'm hearing about it," I said. "What happened?"

"After we got our bid numbers, Bud pulled me aside and said that if I bought that land, *I'd* be the next one planted in the ground."

That was pretty inflammatory, if it were true. "Did anyone else hear him say it?"

"No, he was cagey enough to make sure that there were no witnesses to it," Baron said. "But he said it, mark my words. After I won the land fair and square, something odd happened. I had a hunch that someone was following me around, and when my car broke down at night, I got out to see what was wrong with it. The second I stepped out into the road, someone tried to run me over."

"What did the police say when you told them?"

Baron frowned as he hesitated to reply. "I realize now that it was probably an error of judgment on my part, but I didn't call them. I thought I could handle it myself, but now I'm not so sure."

"It's still not too late to tell the sheriff," I said.

"I don't see how I can do that. I'd just look like I was making it up if I reported it so much later," he said.

I had a hunch that he was making it up right now. There was a ring of insincerity to his story that I just couldn't get past. Why was he trying so hard to get me to look at other suspects? Could it be that he was trying to disguise his own hand in what had happened? "So why are you even telling me? I can't do anything about it."

Jack Baron looked at me long and hard before he said, "If something happens to me, I want somebody to know who was behind it. You solved Cora's murder. If I'm killed, I want you to solve mine, too."

"I'm sure that it's not going to come to that," I said, doing my best to reassure him, though I wasn't at all sure that it was justified. After all, I knew better than most how easy it seemed to be to commit murder. Midnight and Cora had been taken away from me because of greed, so I knew that it could be a motivating reason for some people.

"I'm asking you to step in if it does," Baron said earnestly. "Promise me."

"I'll do my best," I said, not sure how I could turn his plea down without feeling like a waste of a human being. I wasn't a big fan of Jack Baron, but if he died under mysterious circumstances, I'd do my best to figure out what had happened to him.

"That's all that I can ask," he said.

"Why do you think Stick Oakhurst might have done it as well?"

Baron frowned at me before he spoke. "I spoke to Silas not three days before he died, and he told me that Stick was making some threats that he didn't like."

Maybe I'd finally get to the heart of the fight between Stick and Silas. "Did he give you any specific details about their disagreement?"

"No. Silas just said that he'd fix him one way or the other but that he wasn't going to buckle under to bullying. I have a hunch that if Stick kept pushing, Silas might have pushed back, and who knows where that would have led."

"It sounds reasonable enough," I said. "I just wish I knew what Stick was hoping to get out of it."

"You'll have to ask him that yourself," he said.

I decided not to share the fact that I had done just that, without any results. "I'll be sure to do that. While I've got you here, I have a question for you," I said, taking advantage of having one of my suspects right there in my shop.

"What is it?" he asked, doing his best to be warm and inviting. It reminded me of a wolf smiling at a lamb, and I tried to bury my anxiety.

"Did you write Silas a note before he died?"

Jack Baron looked surprised by my question. "A note? What kind of note?"

"It said GIVE ME WHAT I WANT."

"What is that supposed to mean?" he asked me as he frowned.

"I was hoping that you could tell me."

He shook his head. "I don't have any idea what you're talking about." As Baron left the shop, he turned back to me and added, "You need to watch your back, Christy. Something very wrong is going on here."

After he was gone, I considered my options about what I should do next, but I didn't have to make a decision after all.

Thirty seconds after Jack Baron left, Bud Lake burst into the shop. "What did that lying snake say to you just now?"

"Calm down and take a deep breath, Bud," I said.

He ignored my advice. "I won't stand for it, do you hear me? Two different people have told me that he's been going around Noble Point telling folks that I threatened him at the auction and that I killed Silas and Summer. I'll tell you one thing. I'm not going to sit around waiting for Sheriff Kent to put the cuffs on me."

"As far as I know, *nobody's* getting arrested today."

"Well, if I *do* get locked up, I'm suing him for defamation of character or something." After taking a few deep breaths, he added, "I didn't do it, Christy. I never would have killed them. That's what he told you, isn't it?"

"I won't lie to you. Your name did come up in our conversation."

"He's up to *something*, and I know it. Why else would he buy a spread with three trees on it? The man has wiped out more forests than blight and fire combined, so now all of a sudden he wants pasture?"

"He claims that he wants to retire there," I explained.

"That's baloney, and we both know it."

"I'm sorry, but I don't know what to say."

"Say that you believe me, and not him," Bud Lake said.

"I'll be honest with you. At this point I'm not sure *who* to believe," I said.

Bud wasn't pleased with my answer, but at least it was the truth. After a moment, he managed to calm down a little as he said, "If you're looking for a killer, I've got a hunch that you've already found him. I don't know why yet, but I know in my heart that Jack Baron saw something that he wanted, and when he couldn't get it with persuasion, he switched to murder."

"I'd be careful about what I said if I were you," I said.

He looked at me with open contempt. "I'm not afraid of

the likes of Jack Baron."

"Think about it, Bud. If you're right and Jack did kill Summer and Silas, what's to keep him from coming after you to shut you up?"

"Do you want to know the truth? I'd welcome the chance to shoot that rabid fool down in his tracks," Bud said. "We know how to take care of unwelcome varmints on the farm."

"Don't do anything rash, Bud," I said.

"If I act, there won't be anything rash about it," he said dismissively. "Christy, I know you said that you weren't sure who to believe, but I hope that I can trust that you won't spread any of the lies that Jack Baron told you today."

"Or else?" I asked, since it seemed implied by the way he'd just made that last statement.

"I wasn't threatening you," he said, clearly uncomfortable with the entire conversation. "I was just asking you for a favor."

"That's fine, then," I said. "Bud, did you write Silas a note on the day he died?"

My question clearly confused him. "No, I surely didn't. What kind of note?"

"It demanded that someone give them what they wanted," I explained. "Are you saying that it wasn't you?"

"I don't know what you're talking about, so yes, that's exactly what I'm saying. What could I possibly have wanted from Silas while he was alive?"

"I was hoping that you'd be able to tell me that," I said.

"Christy, you need to be careful about what you say."

"What do you mean, Bud?"

He tried his best to smile, but it still looked a little sad. "Not everyone in town is as good natured as I am. If you start going around challenging people about their innocence, you might just give the killer a reason to come after you."

I'd had that exact conversation not ten minutes earlier, and I didn't like it any more the second time. "Let's hope that doesn't happen," I said.

"You don't have anything to worry about from me, but

there's someone with a wicked heart out there doing bad things."

"That's why I'm doing my best to catch them," I said.

"Good enough. I'm glad that we had this little chat."

After he was gone, I wasn't so sure, myself. This was getting too confusing. First Jack Baron had come in explaining why Bud Lake or Stick Oakhurst could have been the killer, and then Bud had followed up with reasons that Jack Baron was the murderer. The problem was that both men had seemed pretty certain that they were right.

Maybe they were, or maybe it had been Jan all along.

One thing was certain; I needed to come up with a new plan if I was going to catch the killer and free Summer's spirit.

I just hoped that she didn't take my cat along with her when she left.

And at the exact same moment that I thought about my ghost cat, Midnight suddenly appeared in front of me, along with his new ghostly companion, Summer.

What was in store for me now?

Chapter 13

"I sure hope that you have some new information for me," I said to the ghostly woman. Then I studied her a little closer. She'd changed somehow, almost becoming more of a solid entity instead of a misty one. "Summer, what's wrong?"

"I don't know," she said, her voice filled with despair. "I can't stay long, Christy. Something is happening to me."

My ghostly cat paced around her, weaving in and out of her legs. It was one of Midnight's ways to comfort his human friends, and he'd done it with me on several occasions in the past. Summer's mood was clearly upsetting Midnight. "If you can describe it to me, maybe I can help." I wasn't at all sure how I could do that, but I was willing to try.

"It's getting harder and harder for me to vanish," she said, the anguish in her words coming through clearly.

"Isn't that a good thing?" I asked.

"Christy, I have a feeling that if you don't free me soon, I'm going to be trapped in this world between the living and the dead forever."

I couldn't think of many things worse than that. "Why is it happening to you?"

"I'm guessing that it's because I lingered," she said simply. "I've had some time to think about it, and that has to be it. I should have Crossed Over when I had the chance, and now I'm afraid that I won't ever be able to."

"Can't you just let go right now?" I asked. I found myself crying for her plight, but I had to wonder if there might be more to it than that. "I promise you that I'll keep looking for whoever killed you and your dad."

"I wish I could, but I've committed to this path. I swore that I wouldn't Cross Over until my murder was solved, and something is holding me to the bargain that I made."

"Are you sure that you can't break it?"

She shook her head. "I don't know how else to explain it,

but I know in my heart that it's a physical impossibility. I can't Cross Over now any more than you can float across the room."

I had a sudden thought that nearly broke my heart. "Is that what happened to Midnight? Is he barred from Moving On because he stayed here for me?" I couldn't stand the thought that my dear, beloved cat would never taste the catnip on the Other Side because of me.

"I don't know why, but I have a feeling that the same rules don't apply to cats." She didn't sound nearly as convincing as I was sure she'd meant to.

"But that's just it. You couldn't possibly know." I got down on my hands and knees and looked straight into Midnight's eyes. "What have I done to you, my friend?"

To his credit, he tried to head-butt me, but he passed right through me. I felt the whisper of a chill as he did, but I couldn't swear that it hadn't just been in my imagination.

"Mrewer," he said, telling me that everything was going to be all right.

I just wished that I could believe him.

After I stood back up, I said, "Summer, I'll work twice as hard to free you. I've already eliminated two of my suspects, so that just leaves four possibilities."

"Four sounds like way too many to me," she said. The expression on her face went from concentration to a sudden and sharp pain. "I'm sorry. I have to go."

And then she vanished.

Midnight lingered. He sat in front of me, gave me one of his most piercing looks, and then he said, "Mrererw."

"I'm doing the best that I can," I answered.

"Mrw." He knew that I was trying. At least that was something.

"Midnight, if you can still Cross Over, you should. Don't stay here for me, for Summer, or anybody else. I know that you love me, but you can't allow yourself to be frozen on This Side. I'd never be able to forgive myself if you were trapped here."

"Mwew," he said, and then my ghostly cat disappeared. I knew that he'd meant to comfort me, but it didn't help.

I might not be able to help him, but I could do my best to find Summer's killer before she froze on This Side.

How exactly I was going to do that, I didn't know just quite yet.

My main focus in life was no longer about making a profit. I knew that my customers wouldn't like it, but I was going to close Memories and Dreams until I managed to track down whoever had killed Silas and Summer. If it meant that I lost the shop, so be it. I took out the one sign I hated to use and hung it in the doorway of the shop. CLOSED UNTIL FURTHER NOTICE. It had an ominous ring to it for me, but I couldn't let Summer be trapped on Our Side just because I couldn't figure out who had killed her and her father.

"Are you free to do a little snooping?" I asked as I called Marybeth while I prepared to close the shop.

"I just pulled up into the driveway," she said. "What's going on? According to my watch, you still have five hours left to work."

"Plans have changed. I'm shutting down the shop until I find Summer's killer." I couldn't tell her why I was in such a hurry to unmask the killer, and I hoped that she didn't ask.

"Why the sudden sense of urgency?"

Of course she'd ask me that. "I have a hunch that if I don't solve it in the next day or two, I'm not going to ever find out who did it."

"Okay, I'm game. Are you coming home, or should I pick you up there?" That was my best friend—ready to help when I needed it, regardless of the circumstances.

"You come here. By the time you show up, I'll be waiting out front."

"Deal," she said. "Let me change out of this suit into blue jeans and a Tee, and I'll be on my way." Marybeth hesitated, and then she asked, "Or would my dress clothes be more appropriate?"

"Jeans are fine," I said.

"Got it," she replied. "See you soon."

After I hung up, I balanced out the register, and then I cleaned it out. Once the cash was safely stashed away in the old safe, I double-checked the door in back, flipped off the lights, and walked out of Memories and Dreams.

As I was dead-bolting the front door, Beth Yates approached. "Are you closing already?"

"I'm sorry. Something's come up." Beth was a regular at the shop, and I hated turning her away, but it was one of those hard choices I had to make.

She studied the sign, and then she turned to look at me. "When will you open back up?"

"I honestly can't say."

She took my hands in hers and looked at me earnestly. "Christy, I know it must be hard running the place after what happened to Cora and Midnight, but you can't give up. We need you."

"I'm not giving up," I said, though I must not have been very convincing.

"Trust me. It will get better. We need you," she said. Beth was one of those people who spoke what was in her heart, regardless of how it might sound. She was one of the sweetest, truest people that I knew, and it was clear that she was doing her best to shore me up.

"I appreciate that more than I can say. I'm really not running away from Memories and Dreams. There's just something that I have to do, and it can't wait."

"You're digging into what happened out at the Bentley farm, aren't you?"

I was surprised by her question. How could she possibly know what I was up to? "What makes you say that?"

"Oh, I hear things," she said with a smile. "Besides, Summer and I went to school together. We were both a little bit odd, so we kind of gravitated toward one another. She was the only thing that made high school bearable for me. When she died, a little something died inside of me as well. It's just natural that I heard you were looking into what happened to her and her father. I never believed that story about carelessness from the start. Anyone who ever spent ten minutes with Silas Bentley knew that the man didn't do anything that wasn't deliberate and well thought out. Can I help?"

"I appreciate the offer, but I can't think of anything that you can do," I said.

"If you come up with something, don't hesitate to call me. I mean that, okay?"

"Okay," I said as Marybeth blew her horn. "I'm sorry, but I've got to go."

"Good luck, and Godspeed," she said.

"Thanks."

I got into the car and buckled up as Marybeth asked, "What was that all about?"

"Somehow Beth knows that I'm digging into Summer's murder," I said. "She even offered to help."

"Good for her. I've always liked that girl. Maybe it's because we share part of our names."

"That's hardly a reason to like someone," I said with a smile.

"You can do worse than trusting a woman with 'Beth' in her name," my best friend said.

"Okay, okay. I got it."

"Good," she said with a smile. "Now, where are we going?"

"We're heading to Tryon's Gap. I want to have another word with Jan Billings."

"It sounds as though you have a plan," Marybeth said as she turned toward Tryon's Gap.

"I don't know if you can call it a plan, exactly," I said. "That sounds more grandiose than it really is. Honestly, it's actually more of a hunch."

"Christy, I'll take your hunches over most people's plans

any day. You've always had a knack for figuring out puzzles."

"I just hope that I'm able to solve this one," I said.

Marybeth took her eyes off of the road for a second to look at me. "This one's really getting to you, isn't it?"

"It is, but I can't tell you why." That was quite literally true, but not for the reason I implied. I knew full well why I couldn't tell her. Maybe someday I could take her into my confidence and explain that Midnight had never left me, but that time was most certainly not now.

"I don't need anything more than that," she said. "If you want to do it, I've got your back."

"I appreciate that," I said.

"So, how do you want to handle Jan? Should we pretend to be on her side, or should we come at her with our guns blazing?"

"I don't think we should be hostile until there's no other option left," I said. "If she didn't kill Silas and Summer, she should *want* to help us find the real killer, right?"

"Right," she said. "Subtle and coy it is, then."

I looked over at her. "Marybeth, you couldn't pretend to be coy to save your life."

"I'd love to be able to deny that, but I'd never be able to keep a straight face."

"At least her car's here," I said as Marybeth finished following my directions to Jan's place and we got out.

"That's got to be a good sign," Marybeth said.

I noticed that the backseat was jammed full of stuff, and the passenger seat up front was overloaded as well. "I suppose so, but based on that car, I'm not sure how long we have to question her."

"All that matters is that we've got her now."

"I'm not going to save anything for later. It looks as though this might be my last chance to question her," I said.

"Give it all that you've got, Christy. I'll stand back and follow your lead."

"Thanks," I said.

Now, if I could just come up with a plan to learn the truth before our feet hit her porch.

Chapter 14

I didn't even have a chance to knock as Jan came stumbling out the front door with her arms loaded down with full paper bags.

"Can I give you a hand?" I asked as she nearly tripped over me.

"That would be great," Jan said. "What are you two doing here?" she asked a little suspiciously as she handed over a few bags.

"Actually, we wanted to talk to you about Silas and Summer," I said, abandoning any thought of subterfuge. It was time for some direct questioning.

"You and the rest of Noble Point," she said as we followed her to her car. After Jan stowed the bags she'd been carrying, she took mine from me and jammed them in as well.

"Who else has been here?" Marybeth asked her.

"Sheriff Kent left not ten minutes ago. He told me that the police believe now that what happened to Silas and Summer wasn't an accident."

So, the sheriff had finally come around to my point of view. That probably wasn't really fair, since I wouldn't have known myself if Summer hadn't told me. "I'm sorry," I said.

Jan slammed the door shut, pinching a few items in the process, but if she noticed, she didn't seem to care. "That makes two of us. It's actually pretty dreadful. In the end, I suppose that it's not that bad a way to go if you have to die anyway. The sheriff said that you just keep sleeping, and most folks don't even realize that they are dying until it's too late to get help."

"I read somewhere that it was a lot worse than that," Marybeth said.

Jan shrugged. "Sheriff Kent told me that it can feel like the flu if you're awake, but if it gets you while you're sleeping, you probably won't even experience any symptoms until you're dead."

"Did he tell you anything else while he was here?" I asked.

"No, but he did ask me for an alibi. I don't suppose I blame him, but it's an unpleasant question to have to answer anyway."

"And did you have one for him?" Marybeth asked her in that oh-so-unsubtle way that she had.

"As it turned out, I did," Jan said. "I was with my boyfriend, Hank, in Charlotte when it happened."

"That must be hard to prove," I said, probing for a weakness in her alibi. "It would all hinge on your boyfriend's word."

"Most nights you'd be right, but I'm a little ashamed to admit that while Silas and Summer were dying up here, I was in a knock-down, drag-out fight with Hank down there. The neighbors called the police, and they wrote up a report when they got there. It was really bad. I realized as I was telling a cop in Charlotte what had happened that it was something I had to end right then and there. I had the officers stay until I packed up my things, and then they waited until I left and came back home." Jan looked upset retelling the tale, and I didn't blame her one bit. It wasn't a very pretty story to have to tell.

Jan continued, "On the drive back here, I decided I was leaving North Carolina once and for all. What happened to the last of my family just cemented it. There's nothing here for me anymore. I'm heading out West for a fresh start."

"Good luck," I said. "I hope that you find what you're looking for." Now that she had a solid alibi, I could extend a little kindness in her direction.

Jan surprised me by hugging me. I hoped that she could tell that I'd meant what I'd said. She was doing something to break a bad pattern, and it took someone very brave to do that, in my opinion.

"Thanks, I really needed that," she said as she pulled away. "I sold my place last night, so this is it. After I drop my keys off with my real-estate agent, I'm gone for good."

She looked back at her home one last time, and it was clear that she didn't have a single ounce of regret. Marybeth and I watched her as she got into her car and drove away.

"So, it appears that we can strike her name off of our list," Marybeth said. "It's a good thing that you closed your shop early. Somehow I doubt that my uncle would have volunteered Jan's alibi on his own."

"It must be tough having the sheriff as family," I said.

"Oh, I don't know about that. It has its perks," she said.

"For example?"

"Well, for one thing, I haven't gotten a parking ticket since he started work," she said, "though I have received more than my share of scoldings."

"So then, it balances out."

Marybeth grinned at me. "I won't pretend that I like being lectured to, but it beats having to pay the fines. What's next?"

"I'd like to talk to Stick again," I said, "but I'm not sure how likely it is that's going to happen. The last time we spoke, I told him I believed that Summer and Silas had been murdered, and he couldn't get away from me quick enough."

"Did he run because he hadn't realized that they had been killed, or because he thought that someone might be trying to tie him to the crime?"

"I wish I knew," I said.

"Then let's go find out, shall we?"

"Stick, are you in there?" I asked a little later after we were back in Noble Point and banging on his front door. His beat-up old pickup truck was parked in front, and I knew that he wasn't about to take off on foot: not given his massive girth.

There was no response to my knocking.

We decided to give it another shot. As I pounded on the front door again, Marybeth called out, "Stick, it's Christy and Marybeth. Come on out so we can talk. We won't bite, I promise."

If Stick was in there, it was getting to be pretty clear that he wasn't coming out.

"Now what?" Marybeth asked me as she tried to peer through a window near the door.

"Well, we can't exactly *make* him come out and talk to us," I said.

"It would be really handy to have a gun and a badge about now, wouldn't it?" she asked me with a grin.

"I don't know about that," I said. "I'm sure that your uncle has quite a few more restrictions on him than we have when we investigate."

"Does that mean that you want to try to break in and *force* him to talk to us?" Marybeth asked excitedly. "Let me find something big enough to throw through a window first," she added as she stooped down to pick up a chipped, painted garden gnome that was guarding the porch.

"You can't do that," I said.

"Sure I can. It's not *that* heavy," Marybeth said as she bounced the gnome in her hands.

"Okay, I misspoke. You *can* do it, but you *shouldn't*."

"I don't see why not," Marybeth said.

"What if he overreacts when we break his window? He could be armed for all we know."

"What if he's gone, though?" Marybeth asked, still holding onto the gnome. "There might be clues lying around all over the place."

"Then what? We can't exactly commit a crime just to try to prove that he might be a killer. If the police come, it won't matter whether you're the police chief's niece or not; we're both going to jail."

That took some of the spunk out of her. Marybeth put the gnome back down, albeit reluctantly. "Then what do we do?"

"We could always just sit around and wait for him to come out," I said.

"I suppose so, but how do we know when that might happen?"

"We don't," I said as I pulled up a chair and sat down. "But do we really have any choice?"

Marybeth took another chair, but after a few minutes, it was clear that she was already bored with our siege. Patience wasn't her strong suit, and I couldn't blame her. Stick had a comfortable place inside, no doubt filled with food, and a bathroom, too. He was in an infinitely better position to wait than we were.

"Christy, I have an idea, if you're willing to try it," Marybeth said in a soft voice.

"You know me. I'm always open to suggestions," I said.

"Let's just pretend to leave. He'll come out, and then we'll pounce on him."

I considered her idea, and then I tuned it up a little. "That sounds good, but how about this? He won't believe that we're gone until he sees your car drive away. We'll make a fuss, and then I'll walk to your car with you. At the last second, I'll jump into those bushes beside the driveway, and you drive away. When he comes out, I'll corner him and talk to him."

It was clear that she wasn't a big fan of my modification to her plan. "So that's all that I'm good for? You're going to just use me as a decoy?"

I grinned at her. "It's better than being the bait, isn't it?"

"Infinitely better," she said with a grin. "Okay, here goes nothing."

"We could always go tackle another suspect and figure out how to deal with Stick later," Marybeth said loudly a moment later. "What do you say, Christy?"

"You're right," I said as I stood. "Let's go see who else we can talk to about what happened at the Bentley farm."

Marybeth started to walk off the porch with me when she changed her mind at the last second and hurried back over to the front door. "Stick, we're leaving for now, but we'll be back later."

As I'd expected, there was no response from inside.

We walked to her car together, and at the last second, I hid in the bushes just as I'd planned and I waited for her to go. Marybeth thought of everything, even slamming her own door twice to make it sound as though we'd both gotten into her vehicle. As she drove down the long driveway, I crossed my fingers and hoped that our plan would work. Otherwise, I had a long walk ahead of me back into town.

Two minutes after Marybeth was out of sight, I heard the front door squeak as Stick Oakhurst stepped tentatively outside to see if we really and truly were gone.

As his foot hit the walkway toward his truck, I stepped out of the bushes and nearly gave him a heart attack in the process.

"Going somewhere, Stick? I hate to tell you this, but we need to talk."

The man looked as though he'd just seen a ghost. Well, good for him. I'd seen them myself, and it wasn't even all that startling to me anymore. "What are you doing here?" he asked.

"Come on. Don't be tedious. I *know* that you heard Marybeth and me knocking earlier. We were certainly not afraid of making noise."

"She's gone, though," he said.

"She might be, but I'm not. Why did you leave the café so abruptly, anyway? Did you kill Silas and Summer? And what were you trying to get from Silas when Summer overheard the two of you fighting?"

"That's a lot of questions," he said a little glumly.

"Take your pick, then. I don't particularly care what order you answer them in, just as long as I get the truth out of you."

"Christy, there are more levels of the truth than you can even imagine."

"Don't get metaphysical on me, Stick. Just tell me what I want to know."

"I don't have to. You need to leave," he said suddenly.

I laughed a little hollowly. I was on shaky ground here, but I couldn't back down now. "Did you honestly think that was going to work? I won't be bullied, Stick."

"If you don't go, I'll *make* you leave," he said as he started toward me. He was a big man, but surely I could outrun him if it came to that. It wouldn't do much for my dignity to be chased down the road by Stick Oakhurst, but that would be a great deal better than dying at his hands.

"Be reasonable," I said as I stood my ground for the moment. "If I have these questions, what do you think other people in town are saying about you?"

Stick frowned at that, and more importantly, he stopped advancing. "Why would anyone be talking about me at all? Have you been spreading lies about me around Noble Point, Christy?"

"Not me, but do you honestly believe that I was the *only* person Summer told about your confrontation with her father?"

"But it didn't have *anything* to do with him dying," Stick said. "That was something else entirely."

"Then why won't you tell me?" I asked. "Trust me, it will feel good getting it off your chest."

He looked as though he was about to say something significant, but then he changed his mind as his shoulders slumped. "You won't believe me. Nobody will."

I was losing him, and I knew it. "Try me. After all, what have you got to lose?"

Stick shrugged. "Quite a bit, actually. I don't *think* that it's related to what happened, but it *might* have been why Silas and Summer died, and that's got me terrified."

This was getting interesting fast. "You've certainly gotten my attention."

Stick looked off in the horizon, and I was wondering if he was gathering the courage to tell me more when I glanced back over my shoulder.

That's when I saw that a police cruiser was making its way up the road. If I was lucky, they'd keep going past Stick's place, but I had a bad feeling that this was exactly where they were heading.

I had to push harder, and I knew that I didn't have much

time left. "Tell me, Stick."

"I'm sorry, but I can't. Christy, you need to go."

"How am I supposed to do that?" I asked as I gestured around the driveway. "Marybeth left me here, remember?"

"That's not my problem." I could see the resolve come back into his face as he straightened up. Where was he finding this new courage? Was it from the looming presence of the police? In a firm voice, Stick added, "All I know is that you're trespassing. You're not welcome here."

"You're making a big mistake, Stick," I said as the police cruiser slowed, pulled off the road, and headed up his lane. I'd been hoping against hope that the car was on its way somewhere else, but I should be so lucky. "You still have time to tell me."

"It's not going to happen," he said as the car stopped and Sheriff Kent got out, looking quite angry.

"Christy, what are you doing here?" he barked out as he approached us.

"She won't leave, Sheriff," Stick said loudly. "I told her that she was trespassing, but she wouldn't listen to me. Can't you make her go?"

The sheriff looked at me for two seconds, and then he commanded, "Get in the car, Christy."

"I don't have to," I said, though I was pretty sure that I did.

His expression softened a bit. "Don't make this any harder than it has to be. I passed Marybeth on my way out here. Wait in the car, and when I'm through, I'll run you back home or to your shop. The property owner has requested that you vacate his land, so my hands are tied. He's within his rights to demand that I remove you."

"Putting her into your car isn't going to be good enough," Stick said. "I want her gone completely."

"Sorry, but the cruiser is going to have to do for now," the sheriff said firmly.

Stick just shrugged at the news. "Just as long as she's not standing right here then."

"She won't be," Sheriff Kent said firmly.

At that point, there wasn't much that I *could* do, so I decided to follow the path of least resistance and do what everyone wanted me to do; I got into the car. But I refused to go into the backseat. That was for criminals. I got in the front and sat on the passenger side, though for one moment I was tempted to sit behind the wheel. That might have amused me, but I was fairly certain that the sheriff wouldn't be too pleased by it.

At least I could roll the window down and hear what they were talking about.

Or so I'd hoped. I was facing the wrong direction though, and I didn't see how I could roll the sheriff's window down without them noticing. I strained to hear their voices, but I couldn't make anything out. It was time for Plan B. Maybe if I watched them, I could at least get a sense of what they were discussing. I saw the sheriff reach into his pocket and pull out a baggie with a piece of paper in it. That had to be the evidence bag that was holding the note that Silas got. *Someone* had written on the back of a grocery receipt the day he was murdered. Did that mean that Sheriff Kent had discovered that Stick had written it, or was he just fishing for a reaction from the man? If he was trolling, he caught what he was after, because as he spoke, I could see Stick's face getting whiter and whiter. The big man kept shaking his head, trying to deny something, but the sheriff wasn't buying it. After a few moments, Stick's expression changed, and I could see him start to talk as the words seemed to bleed out of him. I expected to see the handcuffs come out at any moment, but to my surprise, when the sheriff started back toward the cruiser, he was alone. Stick walked back inside his house a beaten man, and I was left wondering what had just happened.

I just hoped that the sheriff was in the mood to share with me when he got back into the police car. Otherwise, I was going to have to find another way to learn exactly what it was that I had just witnessed.

Chapter 15

"Is there any chance that you'll tell me what he said to you just now?" I asked as the sheriff got in and buckled up his seat belt.

"Christy, can I at least start the car before you start hounding me?" he asked.

"Sure. That's fine. Go right ahead."

"Thank you," he said.

I waited until he started the police cruiser, wheeled it around, and headed down the drive. As a matter of fact, I even waited until he was back on the road toward Noble Point before I spoke again. "What did he say?" I asked again.

"I knew that it was too good to be true," he said. "I shouldn't share information about an active police investigation with you. You know that, don't you?"

"I won't tell anyone if you won't," I said with a grin.

The sheriff just shook his head. "I wouldn't even tell you now if Stick hadn't told me that it would be all right to share it with you. Honest to goodness, I think he's more afraid of *you* than he is of *me*. Why is that, do you suppose?"

"I have no idea," I said. "All I did was try to talk to him."

"I think you just answered my question," Sheriff Kent said.

"Was that the note Jan found that you showed him? It was, wasn't it?"

"It was indeed," the sheriff said.

"Did he admit to writing the threat?"

"No," the sheriff said as he drove. He handled the police cruiser with confidence, as though he were ready and prepared for any contingency, and I didn't doubt that he was. "As a matter of fact, he denied it vehemently until I told him that we had video surveillance footage of him grabbing the receipt out of the grocery store after Silas dropped it."

"Is that true?" I asked.

"We don't fabricate evidence," he said sternly.

It didn't exactly answer my question, but I was in no position to pursue that angle any further. "What did he say when you told him that?"

"He finally admitted it after that," Sheriff Kent said.

"Did he tell you what it was that he wanted from Silas?" I asked.

"He did. It appears that Stick witnessed Silas selling moonshine out of the back of his truck, and so Stick threatened him with exposure if Silas didn't share some of the profits with him."

"Do you believe him?" I asked. I'd heard liquor being associated with Silas by more than one of my suspects, so I had a hunch that it was true.

"I do. We'd been hearing rumors about Silas's side business for a few months now, but we never had any solid proof. After we discovered the bodies, I ordered two of my men to sweep the farm, and they found his still near a spring on the back of his land. It appeared that Silas was having a little trouble making ends meet lately, so he resorted to producing a little liquor on the farm to fatten up his bottom line."

"Could that be why he was murdered?" I asked, seizing instantly on the possibility. "Was he encroaching on someone else's territory?"

"Christy, he didn't butt heads with Al Capone," the sheriff said. "From the size of his equipment, I'd say that he couldn't produce more than a gallon of the stuff a week. That's hardly enough to get anyone else's attention. As a motive for murder, it just doesn't cut it."

I was a little disappointed that the case couldn't be wrapped up right then and there, but I trusted the sheriff's judgment. I had one other thought, though. "What if Stick thought his capacity was much larger? If he's running liquor himself, he wouldn't want any competition at all."

"Contrary to what you might believe, making white lightning isn't for the lazy man," the sheriff said. "Stick wanted a cut of the action, but he wasn't willing to do any work to get it. Besides, he couldn't have killed Silas or Summer."

"Why not?" I asked.

"Because he got into Silas's liquor right after he threatened him with that note. He had time to steal Silas's inventory and drive to Boone, where he proceeded to drink way too much of it and get himself locked up in jail there for being drunk and disorderly. I called it in to the sheriff there, and he confirmed it. Silas would have noticed that hay before he went to bed, so it had to have been stacked after he'd called it a day. I learned early on that the man was a creature of habit, and he never failed to make his rounds before he could rest for the night. Whoever did it struck well after dark."

"I just can't believe that Stick is innocent." I'd convinced myself that he'd been behind it all.

"Well, I'd go a long way from saying that he's innocent of anything, but I'm fairly certain that he didn't kill Silas and Summer."

"Then I'll mark him off my list," I said glumly. If the sheriff was satisfied, and it sounded as though he had every reason to be, then I'd have to accept it as well.

"Who does that leave you now?" the sheriff asked a little too casually for my taste as he pulled up in front of his niece's house, which just happened to be my home as well.

I decided on the spot that I had nothing to lose by sharing with him. After all, the only stake I had in solving these murders was freeing Summer to Move On. If I could help the police trap a killer in the process, so much the better. "I marked Jan Billings off my list earlier today, and from what she told me, so did you."

He nodded. "Hey, I'm just glad that I beat you to one of my suspects before you could get there and question her yourself." He was in a better mood than he'd been in before, and I had to wonder if it had something to do with narrowing his investigation's focus as well.

"I only have two names left on my list," I said candidly.

"Jack Baron and Bud Lake."

The sheriff nodded. "You want to know something? I might have been a little too hard on you earlier."

"Why do you say that?" I asked, honestly curious about his change of heart toward me.

"Both of those names are still viable in my book as well."

"Do you have anyone else that you're looking at?" I asked.

"Let's just say that I'm still investigating all of my leads and leave it at that."

"Okay, we can say that," I said as I started to get out of the police car. I felt a little conspicuous sitting there while our neighbors could see me there. I couldn't imagine the stories that some of them were already making up to spread around town.

"Hang on a second," he said, and I hesitated for a moment. "Christy, you couldn't do me a favor, could you?"

"You know that I can't promise you anything until I know what it is," I said.

"Dial back your investigation for the next twelve to twenty-four hours. There's a good chance this will all be over by then."

That was a pretty big bombshell he'd just dropped. "Would you mind telling me more about what's going on?"

"I would if I could," he said with a loud sigh. "Unfortunately, I can't share anything just yet. What do you say? Will you do that for me?"

I thought about what it might mean to my investigation, and to Summer's spirit, if I cooperated. What if the sheriff was wrong and he was going after the wrong man? Then again, if he was after the *real* killer and I tipped his hand somehow, would I ever be able to forgive myself if *I* was the cause of a murderer going free? I decided that ultimately I couldn't handle that kind of guilt. "I promise that I won't go actively looking for anyone until this time tomorrow, but if someone comes looking for me, I won't run away in the other direction."

"Christy, if one of your suspects comes after you at this

point, that's exactly what you *should* do. You should run as far and as fast as you can, and make sure that you aren't caught."

"I understand what you're saying," I said. It never left my mind that I was playing a dangerous game trying to track down a killer. I knew that whoever I was after had no compunction about killing again, and there was *nothing* more dangerous than a trapped animal. Still, it didn't hurt to be reminded of it every now and then. "I'll stop what I'm doing for now. Would you do me a favor in return?"

"If I can," he said a little uneasily.

"Just tell me how it turns out, one way or the other," I said.

"I can do that. Thanks."

"You're welcome. I should be the one thanking you, actually."

"For the information?" he asked as I closed the door.

"That, and the ride back home."

"I'll be in touch," he said, and then Sheriff Kent drove away.

I'd meant what I'd said, but when those twenty-four hours was up, if he hadn't made an arrest by then, I was going back after a killer.

Where was Marybeth? I'd been expecting to find her back at the house, and I'd been kind of surprised to see that she wasn't there. A sudden thought hit me. Had she gone back to Stick's place looking for me? While the sheriff didn't believe that Stick Oakhurst was a killer, that didn't mean that he wouldn't hurt Marybeth if he felt threatened by her. I could suddenly imagine her lying on the ground helpless with Stick standing over her, and my hands were shaking as I called her cellphone.

She picked up on the second ring. "Hello?"

"Hey, it's me." At least that particular fear had been alleviated. "Where are you?"

Instead of answering, I heard a horn blow nearby, and I looked up to see my roommate and best friend grinning at me as she got out of her car. "I thought Uncle Adam would *never* leave. What were you two talking about so earnestly just now?"

"He's asked me to back off for a day," I said.

"He shouldn't have done that," Marybeth said as she dug her cellphone out of her purse. "We'll just see about that."

"It's okay," I said. "I told him that I would."

Marybeth looked at me with her mouth agape. "You what?"

"He made a reasonable request, and I agreed to it," I repeated.

"Girl, we need to get you inside, because you must have a fever to agree to something like that."

"I'm perfectly fine," I said. "By the way, Stick Oakhurst didn't do it."

"How do you know that?"

"The sheriff just told me," I said.

Marybeth nodded. "Now I get it. You traded him your obedience for some information."

"I wouldn't put it quite that way," I said, offended by the implication that I'd sold out too cheaply.

"Okay, it's not the perfect word for the situation, but that's what it boils down to, isn't it? As far as I'm concerned, it was worth the cost. That just leaves us with two names on our list; the men who fought over the Bentley farm. Do you have any idea which one did it?"

I didn't have to even hesitate before I replied. "They both look guilty to me, but I seriously doubt that they acted together. I just hope that your uncle solves this case soon. The *only* thing I care about at this point is that the killer pays for what he did."

"I couldn't agree with you more," Marybeth said. "So, what are we going to do in the meantime? I don't picture either one of us as the type of gal who just sits around and waits for news."

"No, that's not our speed at all, is it?" I looked at my watch, and I saw that if I hurried, I could reopen Memories and Dreams for the last twenty minutes of my normal hours, but I just didn't feel that it was worth the hassle. Tracking down alibis and uncovering clues was hard business, and I wasn't afraid to admit that I was worn out. "We could order some Chinese food and watch another movie," I suggested.

"Now you're talking," Marybeth said. "Should we invite Lincoln over, too?"

I considered it, but in the end, I suggested, "Let's just make it Ladies' Night, shall we?"

"That sounds perfect to me," she said.

It might be nice to have an actual night off.

But of course, Fate had other plans for me later that evening.

I just didn't know it yet.

Chapter 16

"Should we get our usual meal from The Palace, or should we branch out a little on the menu?" Marybeth asked me as she reached for her cellphone.

"I say we stick to the tried and true," I said.

Before she could dial, though, her phone rang in her hand. "Hello?" she said happily, but the smile on her face vanished quickly. "Yes. Of course. Are you sure? Tonight? Okay, I'll see you there."

"I'm guessing that wasn't a good call," I said as she disconnected the call.

"It was my boss. The company's doing some kind of surprise interviews, and we all have to be in Charlotte in the morning."

"I'm sorry, but at least we've still got this evening."

"I wish," Marybeth said. "That's the second part of the call. Did you hear me say tonight? I'm going to have to take a rain check on dinner and a movie. I have to be in Charlotte in two hours for prep work."

"Is it serious?" I asked. I knew how much Marybeth loved her job, and I'd hate to see her face the possibility of losing it.

"Not for me, but my boss is really worried, and when she has a problem, then so do I."

I followed Marybeth into her bedroom as she quickly packed an overnight bag. "I guess that's one good thing about working for myself," I said. "I don't have anybody to answer to but me."

"Sure, but what can you do when you want to complain about your boss? You'd have to look in the mirror to do it."

"I don't know. I'm not that bad."

"Maybe you're one of the lucky ones after all," she said with a grin. It was amazing how quickly my roommate could pack a bag.

"Wow, you could teach lessons on how to do that," I said.

"Unfortunately, it comes from too much practice in the past." Marybeth latched her bag, and then she tackled her toiletries. In no time at all, she had everything ready. "That's that, then."

"Aren't you forgetting something?" I asked.

She looked around her bedroom, and then Marybeth frowned. "Not that I can think of."

"You aren't going in blue jeans, are you?"

"Of course I am. She's lucky to get me at all. I'm not about to put on a suit just so I can drive two hours. Trust me. She's so worked up that she probably won't even notice *what* I'm wearing. Take care of yourself," Marybeth said as I walked her out to her car.

"Have a safe trip," I said.

"Always," she replied, and then she drove away.

What was I going to do now? I didn't feel like going out, but I was still hungry, and based on what we had in our fridge, if I wanted to eat anything more substantial than peanut butter and crackers, I was going to have to go out to get it.

To my surprise, Lincoln pulled into our driveway before I even made it back inside.

As he rolled down his window, I walked over to him and asked, "What are you doing here? Did we have plans that I forgot about?"

"Not that I know of. I just passed Marybeth on the road. Are you on your own tonight?"

"It looks like it," I said, "but I don't really feel like going out. No offense."

"None taken," he said with a broad grin. "I was on my way home, but I'd be happy to share this with you, if you're interested." He held a pizza box up, and I could smell the cheese and crust from where I stood. "If you have something to drink, you can have half of this. I ordered a medium, but the guy made a large by mistake, so some of this is just going to go to waste."

"I couldn't eat half," I said as I laughed.

"I bet you could if you put your mind to it," he said.

I had to laugh at that. "Come on in. Your offer is too good to pass up."

"Because of the food, or the company?" he asked as he got out of his car.

"Do I really have to answer that?" I asked him with a grin.

"Tell you what. Why don't you *not* answer the question, and I'll supply the answer that soothes my ego the most."

"You men are remarkably fragile creatures sometimes, aren't you?"

"You have no idea," he said.

Lincoln followed me inside, and I quickly set a couple of places at the bar in our kitchen. After getting us both drinks, we settled into our meal as though we'd planned it all along. Lincoln was good company, and I always enjoyed being with him. He'd managed to help me out of my funk after Midnight's untimely, though not permanent, demise, and I knew that I could count on him when I needed him. There were worse suitors I could have had, and I knew it.

He must have caught me staring at him, because he dabbed at his chin with a napkin as he asked me, "Did I get pizza sauce on my face?"

"No, it's not that," I said, and then I pointed to the pizza box as I asked, "This isn't part of your plan to woo me, is it?"

"Believe me; it was purely a coincidence," he said, and then he grinned at me. "Of course, I did take advantage of Marybeth's absence. That's not a point against me, is it?"

"No. As a matter of fact, I'm happy that you came by. I don't feel like being by myself tonight."

He pushed his plate away from him as he smiled. "Well, there's nowhere else that I'd rather be right now than here with you. What else do you have on tap for tonight?"

"Well, Marybeth and I were going to watch a movie," I said.

"Count me in. What are our choices?"

I picked up two videos that Marybeth and I had narrowed it down to earlier. "We've got *While You Were Sleeping* and *Sleepless in Seattle*."

"I sense a theme here," Lincoln said as he studied the cases.

"Romantic comedies?" I asked.

"I was thinking more along the lines of nodding off, but yeah, that, too. Is there any chance you have anything with a little more testosterone in it?"

I thought about our choices, and then I had it. "How about *Mr. and Mrs. Smith*? It's got action *and* romance."

"Sold," he said.

I put the movie in, and as we started to watch, I found my thoughts drifting back to Summer. Being stuck between existences must be horrible, never being able to move forward or back. I hoped that Sheriff Kent was arresting her killer at that moment, but I knew that I wouldn't be able to fully relax until Summer somehow managed to Cross Over.

"Hey, did you hear what I just said?" Lincoln asked me, pulling me out of my fog.

"I'm sorry. I'm a little preoccupied."

"That's okay with me. Should we do this later? I'd be happy to take a rain check."

"You wouldn't mind?" I asked. "I'm not sure that I'll be very good company tonight."

"I doubt that, but I do understand," he said with a smile as he stood. "I'll see you tomorrow, Christy. In the meantime, try to get some rest. Forgive me for saying so, but you look a little worn out."

"Ordinarily I might protest that assessment, but tonight, you're right. I haven't been sleeping well lately."

"It's understandable enough. Is there anything that you'd like to talk about before I go? I've been told that I'm a very good listener."

I thought about telling him about Summer and Midnight, but in the end, I realized just how insane I would have sounded talking about dead women and ghost cats. "Not really."

"Good enough," he said as he kissed my cheek. "Thanks for the company."

"Thank you for dinner," I said.

"It was my pleasure," he said, and then, to my surprise, he hugged me. It felt so good being in his arms that I buried my head into his chest and breathed him in. This was what I missed most about being in a relationship: the gentle embrace of someone who cared for me.

"Hey, are you okay?" he asked as he pulled away thirty seconds later.

"I'm fine," I said. "Why do you ask?"

"Christy, you're crying."

Was I? I touched my cheek, and sure enough, I could feel moisture there. As I wiped the rest of it away, I said, "I'm fine. Really."

"Okay," Lincoln said, though he was clearly perplexed by my reaction. I wasn't about to tell him that I was just as baffled by my tears as he was, but why ruin the mystery? "Was it okay that I hugged you just now? If I crossed any boundaries, I'm truly sorry. It just seemed like the right thing to do at the time."

On impulse, I pulled him to me and kissed him rather soundly.

After we broke it off, he said, "I'm guessing that means that it was all right after all."

I laughed as I pushed him away. "Go home while you're still ahead of the game," I said with a grin.

"You don't have to tell me twice," Lincoln said as he smiled broadly and headed toward his car.

I watched him drive away as it started to rain, wondering what had prompted my reaction to his kindness. In the end, I decided that maybe it was just because I'd felt like kissing him, and for once, I didn't let my inner censor stop me before I acted.

I was still thinking about it when my cellphone rang. Was this the sheriff reporting with news at last? Was Summer's nightmare about to end? All of a sudden my good mood shattered as I prepared myself for the worst.

It was just Marybeth, though.

"Hi," I said, and she must have read something in my voice.

"Wow, you really are bummed that I left, aren't you? Why don't you call Lincoln and see if he can come over?"

"He just left, as a matter of fact, and he even brought me pizza."

Marybeth laughed. "That's better than flowers in my book any day of the week. Since you've got company, I'll let you go."

"I said that he was here," I said. "I didn't say that he stayed."

"He's gone already? Has he given up on wooing you, Christy?"

"No, I believe that's clearly still on," I said as I remembered his hug and then the kiss that we'd shared immediately afterward.

"Then why did you shoo him out so soon?"

I wasn't about to get into that with her over the phone. "Was there a reason for this call, or were just checking up on me?"

"Just checking up," she admitted cheerfully. "Glad to know that you're making do in my absence."

"Come on, I know you better than that. Why are you really calling?"

"You got me. I think I forgot my allergy meds. Would you check my dresser?"

"Sure," I said as I walked through the house toward her bedroom. "There's nothing here," I said after taking a quick look in her medicine cabinet.

"Good, that means that I've got them with me," she said. "Have a good night, Christy."

"You, too," I said.

"Fat chance of that. I'm going to have to hold Maggie's hand half the night. Oh, well. So goes the price of being well paid for what I do."

"What's that like, exactly?" I asked with a smile.

"It's even better than you can imagine," she said as she laughed.

"Bye," I replied, and we hung up.

My hand wasn't even off the telephone when it rang again. If this was Lincoln, I was going to shoot him.

It wasn't, though.

It was the call that I'd been waiting all evening for.

It appeared that Sheriff Kent had news for me at last.

"I'm not disturbing you, am I?" the sheriff asked me after I said hello.

"I've been hoping that you'd call," I said. "What's going on?"

"We're about to make a move on our suspect, and I promised to tell you."

"Who are you going to arrest?" I asked.

"Jack Baron," he said.

"Really? It was Jack? What led you to him?" I asked. I knew that the land developer must have had his reasons, but I couldn't wait to hear what the sheriff had to say.

"It turns out that he didn't want the Bentley farm for his retirement after all," the sheriff explained. "There's a natural-gas pocket on that land. When Silas wouldn't sell the farm to him, evidently Jack took matters into his own hands. His assistant told one of my officers that Baron would do *anything* to get that land, up to and including murder. Now we're going after Baron himself."

"Is that lead really concrete enough to go on?" I asked.

"The gas is real enough, and from what I understand, we'll be getting some direct evidence from his assistant soon. Clearly that man hates his boss with a passion. It worked out helping us though, so I'm not complaining. Listen, I can't really talk. I just wanted to keep my word to you."

"Thank you," I said.

After I hung up the phone, I felt let down by the outcome. Was it because the resolution of the case was happening somewhere else without me, or was there another, more dire reason? What if they were going to arrest the wrong man? It was nonsense, and I knew it, but I still couldn't keep myself from feeling as though the sheriff was about to make a big mistake. It was like when I flipped a coin and found myself hoping for one outcome more than the other. I didn't fully realize that Bud Lake was the killer until I heard from the sheriff that he was arresting Jack Baron. But did I have any proof?

One thing that I hadn't considered before was that Jack wasn't all that familiar with the ins and outs of the farm. Could he have known how to disable that heater, or to stack a bale of hay next to the exhaust to block it? I doubted that he would know either fact, but another farmer probably would, especially one who was right next door to Silas and Summer. Bud Lake could probably traverse that distance with ease, even in the dark, whereas Jack would probably get lost in the darkness. I knew that greed could be a powerful motive, but a dead child was probably the strongest one anyone had ever felt. No matter how much Bud had downplayed what had happened to his son, I knew that it had left a crushing hole in his heart. I didn't have many facts to back up my hunch that the sheriff was going after the wrong man, but my gut hadn't let me down yet, and I was going to trust it this time, too. If I could just talk to Bud again, I might be able to trip him up, but I'd promised the sheriff twenty-four hours.

That was before he'd been moving in on an arrest, though. Surely that freed me from my promise to him to stand idly by. What was the worst thing that could happen if I went to talk to Bud? I'd make a fool of myself, something that I could live with if I had to.

And the best thing that could happen?

That had to be that the real killer would be caught soon, and hopefully in time for Summer to Cross Over before she was trapped between worlds forever.

Chapter 17

But I wasn't about to tackle Bud alone.

Lincoln was clearly surprised to get my phone call. "What happened, Christy? Did you miss me already?"

"Something like that. What are you doing right now?"

"I can come over, if that's what you're asking." He sounded a little too eager, and I wondered if I'd been premature with that kiss.

"Actually, I was hoping that you could meet me out at Bud Lake's farm."

"Is he the one?" Lincoln asked, all of the playfulness suddenly deserting his voice.

"The police don't think so, but something is bothering me about the man. I just can't put my finger on it. So, what do you say? Are you interested?"

"I'll be there before you are," he said.

"Challenge accepted," I said, happy that I'd called Lincoln as backup. I didn't *need* a man to protect me, but that didn't mean that I should rush off into what might turn out to be a dangerous situation without planning ahead for contingencies. "I'll see you there."

"I'm looking forward to it," Lincoln said, and then we hung up.

I felt a little foolish calling him as I drove through the rain toward Bud Lake's place, and I thought about calling him and canceling, but for some reason, I couldn't bring myself to do it. I had to turn my wipers on their fastest setting to clear the windshield, but by the time I got to the Lake place, it had eased up a little.

Where was Lincoln, though? As I approached the house, I looked around for his car, but I couldn't see it anywhere. Pretty soon, I was going to have to make a choice. I could go it alone and hope that he showed up before I got myself into trouble, or I could wait by the road for him. If I parked at the edge of Bud Lake's driveway, he wouldn't be able to get out without me moving my car first, so in essence, he would be trapped. Finally, I decided to give Lincoln four more minutes to get there. If he didn't show up by then, I was going in without him.

The digital clock on my dash seemed to crawl as one minute replaced the last, but finally Lincoln's four minutes were up.

I crept up the driveway slowly, hoping that reinforcements would arrive before I got there, but I was finally at the house, and there was still no sign of Lincoln. Now what? I could always pull off to one side of the driveway and wait for him. The rain was coming down harder again, so I could use that as an excuse if Bud noticed my car. I'd just about decided to wait, no matter how long it took, when a large flashlight tapped on my window, nearly scaring the life out of me.

Bud was standing there, his flashlight in one hand and his raincoat held over his head with the other. "What are you doing out here, Christy?"

"I came by to see you," I said as I rolled down the window a little, letting some of the rain fall inside.

"Then come on in," he said as he gestured toward the house.

I really had no choice at that point. I threw the hood of my raincoat over my head and dashed for the front porch behind Bud. By the time we were out of the rain, we were both soaked, our jackets proving to be pretty ineffective against the deluge. "Come on inside and dry off. You can warm up and tell me what this is all about."

I searched the road behind me again, but there was still no sign of Lincoln. What could possibly have happened to the man? Was he the one who was in trouble now? I envisioned him on the side of the road trapped in a wrecked car because of the rain, and I felt sick that if it were true, it would be all my fault.

If something happened to him, I'd never be able to forgive

myself.

Bud hung his jacket on a hook by the door, and I hung mine beside it. "Let me grab a couple of towels for you, Christy. I'll be right back. In the meantime, warm yourself up."

He pointed to a familiar-looking heater, and I walked toward it before I realized where I'd seen its twin.

It was identical to the one in Silas's place.

That was how Bud had known about the vent and how to rig the heater up for the safety to fail. I knew that odds were good that Jack Baron would have no idea how to make the heater malfunction or just where to stack hay to cut off the exhaust vent. I had a sudden hunch that the sheriff had gotten this one wrong. I only hoped that I lived long enough to tell someone what I'd found. As I reached for my phone to call the police, Bud walked back into the room. "Who are you calling, Christy?"

"Lincoln was supposed to meet me here," I said. "I just want to check and see what's going on with him."

Bud grinned at me, but there wasn't any warmth in it. "Well, you'll never get a signal out here, at least not when it's raining. It's iffy on a good day, and we both know that it's far from that out there right now."

"He'll be along soon, at any rate," I said.

"As a matter of fact, I don't believe for one second that he will," Bud said. "You know the truth, don't you?"

"About what?" I asked, doing my best to feign ignorance.

"There's no use denying it. You'd make a terrible poker player. I wanted to see your reaction to the heater to see if you recognized it, and you surely did. When did you see the one at Silas's place?"

"On the day of the auction," I said, remembering how I'd noticed it when I'd been looking at Ginny's costume jewelry.

"It might not have been the smartest thing I ever did inviting you in just now then, was it?"

"I won't tell a soul," I said. "I promise." Where was my backup? Lincoln had *better* be hurt, because if he wasn't, and if I somehow managed to survive this confrontation, I was going to kill him.

"As much as I'd like to take your word on it, I'm afraid that I can't trust you." He reached between two towels and brought out an old handgun, its handle taped together with shiny gray duct tape and its barrel clearly showing signs of rust. Would the thing even fire? The real question was if I were willing to take the chance that it wouldn't.

"Was it all because of your son?" I asked him, hoping to stall for a little time.

"That boy was all that mattered to me in the world, and Summer took him away from me. She sealed her own fate the day she came back into town and put herself in my reach again. It was Fate that put her that close to me, and I wasn't about to miss out on another chance to make things right."

"Did it help, Bud? Did killing Silas and Summer bring you one ounce of satisfaction?" It probably wasn't a brilliant move on my part to antagonize the man, but if I was about to die, I honestly wanted to know the answer to that.

"Not so much," he admitted, "but I have to play this out. If I go to jail in the end, then so be it, but justice has been done."

"Silas died, too," I said. "You two used to be friends."

"That was a lifetime ago. He took his daughter's side, and there wasn't a thing that I could do about it. Now, you'd better grab your coat. You're about to have yourself a little accident."

I nodded, pretending to be obedient as I reached my jacket. Bud wasn't very experienced at this, and he let me get too close to him *and* the gun he was holding on me. I whirled my jacket in his face, and the next instant, I felt my hair flip up as the bullet nearly took off a chunk of my scalp. That gun might have looked like a piece of junk, but it could still shoot.

I had to get out of there while I could. I burst out the front door and started running toward the road. For a split second, I'd considered getting in my car and driving off, but Bud was too close behind me.

My only chance was on foot.

I raced out into the night, and just before what sounded like a clap of thunder exploded behind me, I tripped on something that I couldn't see.

As I fell, another bullet whizzed past me.

The rain was beating down heavily again, but I could barely feel it on my skin. I looked to see what had tripped me, and as I did, a ghostly hand vanished in the rain, as though it were made of cotton candy. Summer had just saved my life, but I wasn't at all sure that she could save me again. The problem was that Bud could see me in the muted light coming down from the road. I decided that the open field was my best chance, so I swiftly changed direction and headed for a darkened patch in the night. As I ran, I realized that it *had* to be the barn. Maybe I could get in and lock the door, if I could make it there in time. At least I had a fighting chance locked inside. Out in the rain, I was as good as dead. I'd long given up on Lincoln. Something had happened to him, and I was on my own now.

I heard a curse behind me, and I looked back just as Bud started swearing at the gun in his hand. At least the thing had finally misfired. I slipped in the mud a few times, but I finally made it into the barn. There were tools scattered all over the place, but I went straight to a pitchfork much like Lincoln had bought at the Bentley auction not that long ago. It had a good heft to it, and I stood there at the door braced and ready for Bud Lake to come through.

With any luck, he would soon find himself impaled on his own work tool.

Bud clearly had other plans, though. As I stood there waiting for him, the lights in the barn all came on at once, throwing the place in sudden bright light, and I turned at the sound of his voice. He'd slipped around the back and caught me completely by surprise. The way that I figured it, his gun beat my pitchfork in every scenario I could play out in my mind.

"Drop it, Christy," he ordered. I wasn't the only one who must have fallen to the ground during our chase. There was a gash on his forehead, and he was bleeding quite freely from it. Bud's clothes, once neat and clean, were now a muddy mess, just as mine were.

Instead of letting the pitchfork down easily, I drove it into the barn's dirt floor. It stuck up defiantly, as though it were daring Bud to follow through with his plan to murder me, too.

"I'm afraid that you're going to have to suffer a little for putting me through that," Bud said. He didn't sound nervous at all, but I was shaking wildly. I wasn't ready to die yet. It didn't matter that I had my own evidence that at least some of us Crossed Over.

Just because Summer could have didn't mean that option would be open to me when I was gone.

"Don't do it, Bud. It's not worth it," I said, fighting to keep my voice from quivering. I might be about to die, but I wasn't about to give him the satisfaction of knowing that I was scared out of my mind.

"It might not be, but it's all that I have left. Good-bye, Christy."

I started to close my eyes. I really didn't want to see him kill me, but something inside wouldn't let me turn away or shut my eyes. If Bud was going to shoot me down in cold blood, then he was going to have to do it staring straight into my defiant eyes.

I braced myself for the shot, and then, out of nowhere, the lights suddenly went out. Was it my guardian ghost acting to save me again, or had something within the storm knocked the power out? Either way, I wasn't about to lose the opportunity to live through this.

I reached for where I thought the pitchfork must be, but in the darkness, I couldn't find it! Where had the blasted thing gone? I started stumbling around searching for it when the lights came back on. "Give it up, Bud," I heard Lincoln say as he approached Bud Lake's back, and I'd never been so happy to hear someone else's voice in my life.

The only problem was that Lincoln didn't have a gun on him. He did have a tire iron, but it wasn't going to be any more successful at saving us than that pitchfork had been in my hands.

"Look out! He's got a gun!" I shouted as Bud whirled around to face Lincoln. I saw the pitchfork next to me, and I grabbed it in what felt like one easy motion. Before Bud Lake could shoot Lincoln, I threw the pitchfork like a javelin straight at his heart. It turned out that my aim was true, but I wasn't as strong as I'd hoped. Instead of hitting Bud in the side, or maybe even the arm holding the gun, it dropped in its flight until I was afraid that it wasn't even going to reach him at all.

And then I watched it strike home as the farthest tine dug into his big toe, drawing blood.

The gun went flying as Bud fought to remove the pitchfork that had suddenly sprouted from his foot, and Lincoln and I both dove for it before Bud Lake could free himself.

Chapter 18

As Lincoln recovered the gun, Bud finally managed to free himself. He wasn't in the clear, though. His shoe quickly started spilling blood, and I wondered if there was some kind of artery down there that I didn't know about.

"Don't move," Lincoln commanded him, but Bud dropped to the ground anyway and tore off his shoe.

"She tried to kill me with that thing!" he yelled loudly, something that I found hysterically funny for some reason.

"By all rights, I should get another try," I said with strange laughter in my voice. "After all, you shot at me twice." I paused, and then I added, "Three times, if we count that misfire." I looked over at Lincoln, who was watching me with a worried expression. "Don't you think that should count?"

He nodded, and then he said, "Christy, call the sheriff."

"I would, but Bud already told me that there's no signal here in the rain." I was being rather calm about things all of a sudden, and I had to wonder if perhaps I was in shock.

"Then take out your keys, get into your car, and drive until you get a signal. When you've got one, call the sheriff," he instructed. "Can you do that, Christy?"

"Sure I can," I said, though I made no move to go anywhere.

"Now would be nice," Lincoln said.

I suddenly snapped out of it. "Got it. I'll be right back." Before I opened the door, I turned and looked back at Bud, who was still trying to stop the blood flow coming from his foot with a ratty old bandana. "Don't you go anywhere now, you hear me?"

He said something that wasn't worth repeating, so I took off back out into the rain. I half expected Summer and Midnight to be with me, but I made that cold and wet walk alone, and the drive to a spot with better reception as well. Was Summer already gone, then?

It took me a few minutes to explain to the sheriff what had happened, but once I made myself understood, he acted pretty quickly. "Don't do anything. We'll be right there. Christy, I'm sorry."

"You shouldn't be apologizing. You didn't do anything," I said.

"I let you down," he said.

"Just get here as quickly as you can," I said, and then I purposefully shut off my phone. I couldn't stand the thought of talking to anyone else.

By the time I got back to Lincoln, Bud had made a tourniquet of sorts out of his bloody bandana. It looked as though he was going to make it. Why didn't I care more about that than I did?

Once Lincoln was relieved by one of the deputy sheriffs, he wrapped me up in his arms. "Are you okay?"

"He never touched me," I said numbly. "How about you?"

Lincoln shrugged. "I tore up one of my knuckles changing a tire. That's what kept me. It was pretty bad trying to swap that thing out in the rain."

"But you kept trying until you got it, didn't you?" I asked. "Good for you."

"You didn't do so bad yourself," he said. The paramedics followed soon after the police, and Lincoln wouldn't let them even look at Bud until they'd checked me out. I got a blanket, a quick examination, and *then* Bud got his toe looked at.

The sheriff managed to get a moment alone with me before we all left Bud Lake's property. "Sorry I was wrong about Jack Baron," he said.

"I was wrong, too. I didn't realize that the heaters were the same at both places until Bud practically pushed me into his. If you ask me, I have a feeling that he *wanted* to get caught. The guilt must have been too much for him to take."

"Not enough to keep him from trying to kill you, though," the sheriff said with a wry grin.

"What do you know? It turns out that killing me is tougher than it looks."

"And a good thing that is," the sheriff said. "I can take you home myself, and one of my people can follow you in your car."

"If it's all the same to you, I'd just as soon drive by myself," I said. "I need some time to process all of this."

Lincoln had been listening in. "Don't worry. I'll follow her home, Sheriff," he said.

"You can drive behind me to make sure that I get there safely, but I'm going in alone." I was being stubborn about it, but not for the reasons I'm sure they were assuming. If Summer was still around, she wouldn't appear if anyone else was there.

I had to know, one way or the other, if I'd been in time.

"That's fine," Lincoln said, and that's exactly the way that it all worked out. I didn't realize how tightly I was wound until I walked across the threshold of the home I shared with Marybeth. Once I was back there, and safe at last, I felt the tension flow out of me.

And then I saw a flickering light in the hallway.

Was it Summer and Midnight, or had I just gone the rest of the way around the bend?

With what appeared to be great difficulty, Summer appeared in the next moment, but it wasn't all at once, which had been her custom up until then. Instead, it was gradual, as though she was expending great energy to show herself to me, even with Midnight's help.

"You're alive," she said with great relief once she was fully formed again. That was a tricky term, since her composition still appeared to be in a misty state to me.

"Thanks to you," I said. "You tripped me, didn't you?"

She looked a little upset by my comment. "It was the only way that I could get you out of his line of fire."

"I'm not complaining," I said. "If you hadn't grabbed my leg when you did, I would have been a goner. How did you even manage to do it?"

"It cost me, I won't deny it, but I had no choice, did I? You did it all trying to help me."

I was sorry that I had caused my new friend pain, but there was nothing that I could do about it. "We got him, Summer."

"Are you certain?" she asked, as though she couldn't trust herself to believe that it was really true.

"Bud Lake confessed to killing you and Silas."

"Because of what happened to David," she said sadly.

"I'm afraid so. He just couldn't let it go. But Summer, think about what that means. You can Cross Over now."

"If only it were that easy," she said.

I felt my heart sink. "Does that mean that you're stuck here? Is it because of the way that you saved me? I can't live with myself if that's true."

"I don't know why, but it's just too hard now. I'm afraid that this will be the last time that I'll be able to make myself seen even by you. Midnight gives me a great deal of strength, but it's just not enough anymore."

"You can't give up," I said, pleading with her. "You have to try."

"I have been," she said. "I'm afraid that it's no use."

I looked squarely at my cat, who was listening intently to our conversation. "Help her, Midnight. You can do it. I know that you can."

"Mrwerer," he said defiantly. I knew that tone of voice all too well.

"You have to at least try," I answered.

Midnight stretched out his neck, and then I could swear that my sweet ghostly cat nodded at me and winked. Surprising us both, he leapt to his feet and jumped straight at Summer. Summer was clearly caught off guard by the sudden action, and she instinctively tried to put up her hands to protect herself from his impact. When the two of them touched, the light in the room suddenly brightened to double its normal intensity, and I could swear that I could hear a rumble tear through the room as they made contact.

And then, to my dismay, I was all alone.

Summer had managed to Cross Over, but at what cost?

It appeared that Midnight had sacrificed his halfway existence to help her along in her journey, at my urging, and now he was gone too, for what was probably going to be forever.

It was more than I could stand.

I fell to the floor, weeping with uncontrollable sorrow and sadness.

I hadn't realized just how much I'd grown to depend on the chance that I might see Midnight come around the corner again until it was gone.

And now I'd never felt more alone in my life.

Chapter 19

I managed to crawl into my bed, but that was all of the energy that I had left in me. Shadow was upset about what he'd witnessed as well, but there was nothing that I could do to comfort him at the moment.

My own heart was breaking all over again.

And then I heard the loveliest sound I'd ever heard in my life.

"Mrrwerer."

I pulled the blankets off my head and found myself inches from Midnight's ghostly face.

"You're here," I said, and then, without even thinking about it, I tried to hug him. My hands went through him, of course, but he didn't seem all that unhappy about my attempt to make contact with him. "What about Summer? Did she make it?"

"Mrer," he said, which sounded exactly like "of course" in feline chatter.

I didn't want to say what I felt that I had to next, but I owed it to my dear friend. "Midnight, if you need to go, I completely understand. I don't want you to get stuck here because of me."

"Phht," he said, a noise he reserved especially for when he thought I'd lost my mind, which had happened more than I'd liked when he'd still been alive.

"Does that mean that you can stay a little longer?"

"Mrer," he said. Of course.

It was all that I needed, and more than I had any right to expect.

After seeing my smile, Midnight floated off the bed and went out into the hallway, in search of his former companion, no doubt. He and Shadow had formed an easy alliance after his return that had surprised me, though that was truly a difficult thing for either one of my cats to do after the years we'd spent together.

And now it appeared that we'd have more time left after all.

I wasn't at all certain just how long I'd have Midnight with me, but that didn't matter.

What mattered was that I had him with me right now.

Printed in Great Britain
by Amazon.co.uk, Ltd.,
Marston Gate.